RED SPIKES

RED SPIKES

MARGO LANAGAN

ALFRED A. KNOPF
New York

THIS IS A BORZOI BOOK PUBLISHED BY ALFRED A. KNOPF

This is a work of fiction. Names, characters, places, and incidents either are
the product of the author's imagination or are used fictitiously. Any resemblance to
actual persons, living or dead, events, or locales is entirely coincidental.

Copyright © 2007 by Margo Lanagan

Published in the United States by Alfred A. Knopf, an imprint of Random House
Children's Books, a division of Random House, Inc., New York. Originally published
in Australia by Allen & Unwin.

KNOPF, BORZOI BOOKS, and the colophon are registered trademarks of Random House, Inc.

www.randomhouse.com/teens

Educators and librarians, for a variety of teaching tools, visit us at
www.randomhouse.com/teachers

Library of Congress Cataloging-in-Publication Data
Lanagan, Margo.
Red spikes / Margo Lanagan. — 1st American ed.
p. cm.
Originally published in Australia by Allen & Unwin in 2006.
ISBN 978-0-375-84320-4 (trade) — ISBN 978-0-375-94577-9 (lib. bdg.)
[1. Supernatural—Fiction. 2. Interpersonal relations—Fiction. 3. Australia—Fiction.
4. Short stories.] I. Title.
PZ7.L216Red 2007
[Fic]—dc22
2007004805

Printed in the United States of America
October 2007
10 9 8 7 6 5 4 3 2 1
First American Edition

CONTENTS

RED SPIKES

Baby Jane

"Well, at least it's a fine night," said Mum.

She looked enormous, but that was mostly the bedding she'd gathered as she hurried out of the hut. Her hair, coming undone from its nighttime tail, was a shock of silver on her shoulders.

"Though how we'll sleep with this moon I don't know. It's like the floodlights at the Cricket Ground. We need to find a place in the shade. Not under these gums, though—if they drop a branch, we're dead. Down by the creek there, among the casuarinas—"

A bellow interrupted her. Everyone looked up at the hut. Mum walked away down the hill, trailing a corner of the quilt across the moon-white grass. "And a good distance from *that*.

That could go on for hours. Days. Come on, everyone, let's get settled."

Dylan followed her slowly. She wasn't acting right. Anything to do with babies and births, Mum usually took over. She became queenly herself, moving differently, spreading a radiant peacefulness all around. She paused the world so the baby could land on it safely. Yet here she was, *walking away* from a woman in labor.

"I think we should get the *police*," grumbled Ella, lumbering down the slope. She was pregnant, too; she was what Mum described as *about ready to drop*. "It's outrageous. Whoever heard of it? Where did those people escape from—some kind of costume party?"

Todd gave an enormous yawn. "Dunno what you're moaning about—you weren't asleep anyway. You *never sleep*, remember? 'S what you're always saying."

"I *do* never sleep," said Ella. "Not these days. Or nights."

The family moved down the slope ahead, in among the darker trees. They weren't nearly alarmed enough; that must be part of the magic. Dylan was panting, as if his body were trying to pump out the strong, wet-grass smell of bear and replace it with the proper bush smells of eucalypt and pine.

"Check for sleeping snakes," Mum said when they reached the creek side, where the ground was flatter. "Bang about a bit."

So everyone stamped around in their pajamas. It would have been funny if Dylan hadn't been so frightened. Weren't they *worried* about that bear? Weren't they *upset* about what had happened? It was eerie that they were positioning air mattresses and spreading blankets and plumping pillows. Titch and Edwin were already asleep—look at them. They hadn't even cried. It was all a dream to them. Dylan pinched the inside of his elbow hard; he rubbed his arm roughly against a tree trunk; he breathed in and stared at the frills of white water along the creek, at the shadow people and the shadow trees, at the millions of stars above among the needly casuarina twigs. He smelled the smoke from the hut chimney. That funny man must be building up the fire. You needed boiling water when a baby was coming. What for? Dylan couldn't remember.

"Come on, Dylan. Come and settle down between Dad and me. We'll protect you against jibber-jabbers." Her smile was the only part of her face that was moonlit.

"Jibber-jabbers," said Dad dozily. "That's going back a long way. What were those things, anyway, Dyl? You never told us properly; you were too scared even to talk about that nightmare."

Dylan crawled up the valley between them, laid his head in the pillow cleft, and shuddered. "They were these horrible creatures, hundreds of them, about up to my shoulders. They had big heads, big jaws, lots of teeth. *Jibbrah-jibbrah*, they said, *jibbrah-jibbrah-jibbrah-jibbrah*. They rushed at me out of the wardrobe and snapped their teeth."

Dad snored gently.

"I still don't like to think about them," Dylan said to Mum.

"Don't, then," said Mum comfortably. "I don't know where they came from in the first place—some movie? None of the others had such night terrors." She closed her eyes with decision. She always knew what to do. Dylan tried to be as firm about closing his.

They had rushed at him, jabbering, their eyes glowing yellow among the spines. And then a worse noise, a terrible rough growl, had stopped them, made them cringe, made them jabber quieter, at each other instead of at him. *Zing!* Someone had drawn a sword, over by the wardrobe.

Then a white flash, and a snap, and they'd gone, and Dylan was sitting up in bed staring at the wardrobe and yelling into the empty room.

Now, he buried himself deeper between Mum and Dad.

The creek rustled and chuckled and blipped.

Todd farted musically.

Ella said, "To-odd!"

"What's your fuss? We're out in the open air, aren't we?"

Mum gave a little laugh through her nose, and Dylan let his giggle out.

"Shh, now." Mum turned on her side so that her face was out of the moonlight.

Dylan followed the shadow line of her profile, from silver-fringed forehead along to soft under-chin and lace nightie collar. Nothing could seriously go wrong with the world while she hung there, could it? Or while Dad's back was all up and down his own?

He thought he heard a sound from the hut, through the creek noise. He tipped his head so that both ears were free to listen. His body had tensed; he tried to go floppy again.

"Still, Doug . . . ?" said Mum.

Dad made an unwilling sound.

"He's asleep," whispered Dylan.

"Hmm."

Dylan waited for her to speak again, but she didn't. "What were you going to say to him?" he whispered.

"It is odd, isn't it?" she whispered.

"It's *very* odd. It's really, really, *really*—"

"I mean, who are they? How come we just let them— Where did they come from?"

Dylan lay there awhile. He breathed and she breathed, and when he thought, from her breath, that she was possibly asleep, he whispered, very quietly, "I found them."

She lifted her head. "You found them?"

He nodded. The moon jiggled in the tree.

"When? On your walk this afternoon? Up on the mountain?"

He shook his head. "When we were playing hidey. In among the rocks over there." And he pointed above his head, across the creek.

"What, they've been lying low in the rocks?"

"It wasn't hard for them to hide," said Dylan. "They were only this big." He showed her with his thumb and forefinger. "Stiff, you know, not moving. On bases, like those soldiers Uncle Brett paints."

He had held the little figures in his hand in the sunlight, waiting for Aaron to find him. He had admired their detail, the pregnant queen's fierce face and helm, the bear whose every hair seemed to have been molded separately. Its claws actually dug into Dylan's skin—he must make sure the littlies didn't get hold of these. These were like Uncle Brett's soldiers; they were *not toys*. And the funny bald servant man, all hung about with bags and equipment—something about his face, Dylan just knew he was going to up and *complain*.

Mum still hovered there.

"So I put them in my pocket," Dylan said. "And when I got changed for bed, I put them under my pillow."

"And in the night they . . . expanded?"

"Yes. Came to life."

And the bed had broken under their weight, and Dylan had tumbled off the stinking bear, and then the queen struck him aside with a gauntleted hand (he rubbed the welts on his cheek), and the little bloke's bald head rose against the window and said some foreign words anxiously. The queen exclaimed and raved and waved her daggers about. The bear made an irritated noise on a blast of clover breath, and then the man's voice, which was high-pitched, almost like a woman's, said clearly, "Please vacate the room. The queen requires complete privacy."

And here they were. Auntie Rachel and the others in the tents hadn't even woken up. The *dog* hadn't even woken when they filed out past its basket on the veranda: Mum and Dad, Ella and Todd, Ed and Titch and Aaron and, last of all, Dylan.

All around him the sleepers breathed. The creek chuckled by. Mum's head sank to her pillow.

"Well, I don't understand it, Dyl," she said. "I have to believe you, because you're hopeless at lying, but a *bear*? And that woman with the armor on? Whoever heard of maternity armor? It's got me beaten. I daresay it'll all come clear in the morning, though, even the bear. It'll be her husband or something, in a bear suit—one that needs a good dry cleaning. Didn't it *stink*!"

And she had talked herself, and Dylan, to sleep.

A high, anxious voice woke him. Dylan lifted his head. The bald manservant was walking, bent and hesitant, among the sleeping family. He held something to his mouth, some kind of magnifying glass, only without the glass, and he spoke through it.

"Can anyone help?" he said. "My queen is in difficulties. Is there a midwife here? Any kind of leech, any wise woman? Please, my queen is in great pain." And indeed, the bellowing from up the hill was rawer and more desperate now.

"You want my mother," Dylan said as the man came close. "She knows what to do at births." He rocked Mum and patted her head as he spoke.

"She does?" said the man. Another instrument gleamed at the man's ear, and his lips moved differently from the words Dylan heard, as if he were in a dubbed movie. "Then she is just the person we need. Bring her up to the hut immediately," he said, suddenly imperious. "I must return to my lady's side."

But Mum wouldn't wake. Dylan shook and shook her; he tweaked her hair; he pinched her cheeks; he held her nose and covered her mouth. She batted him away—"Don't *do* that!"—but her eyes didn't open, and as soon as she could breathe again, she was deeply asleep.

The queen's roaring went on.

"Come on, Mum!" Dylan shouted into her ear. "Come and help with this baby! Mum, it's Dylan! Wake up and help!"

She didn't move. Her eyelids didn't even tremble. It was useless.

Dylan stood up. No one else had woken up, either; no one was going to. They were all magicked asleep, or weirded asleep. Whatever had to be done, *he* would have to do it.

He picked his way among the bodies and uphill over the stones and tough grass. At the top, the veranda shaded the mad face of the hut, two yellow window-eyes and a gaping door-mouth. He didn't know what the queen was saying, but there was so much rage in it that it must be swearing.

He climbed the stairs even more slowly. The bear's head was in the doorway—so big!—licking something off the floor. Dylan peered in, hoping the bear would move aside. The manservant wept and clasped his hands at his mouth, beside the roaring stove. A chain slung over one of the rafters held up a very dirty foot—

"Oh, there you are!" The servant hurried to the door. "Out of the way—move, brute!" He pushed the bear's head aside with his foot. He frowned into the darkness beyond Dylan. "Where is she?"

"She wouldn't wake up."

"Fetch her, fetch her!"

"It's no good," said Dylan. "Whatever brought you here knocked everyone out. Put everyone to sleep. We'll have to manage without her."

"And are you a midwife, too?" The servant looked him up

and down. Dylan felt less than impressive in his gold polyester boxer shorts.

"Well, I've seen some babies born. And Mum and Ella, they've been talking nonstop about births for the last couple of months. And I can tell you right off, your queen is in the wrong position."

"What are you talking about? She's in *exactly* the right position!"

Dylan edged in around the bear's head. The floor was sticky—the bear had torn open a squeeze-pack of golden syrup and was spreading it thinly and widely with its tongue. Now he could see the whole of the struggling queen. She was flat on her back on the table, with her feet chained high and wide, and her arms tethered with a leather strap that ran under the tabletop. *The stupidest position*, Mum always grumbled when she saw it on television. *Flat on her back for the convenience of some doctor.*

"What have you got her like that for?" Dylan heard Mum's voice come out of himself. "How's gravity supposed to help her there?"

"I know nothing of this *Gravity*. It is always done like this at court," said the manservant angrily. "Look, here are the tools, all laid out according to the lore."

Dylan had never seen instruments like these before. They looked very specific and very brutal—and very dirty. *That* was what the boiling water was for—for the midwife's instruments, to sterilize them.

"Well . . . well, you're not at court now, are you? Get her feet down!" cried Dylan over the queen's noise. He took one of the daggers from the queen's belt and cut the table strap. Immediately she grabbed both his upper arms and raved loudly, urgently, into his face.

The manservant fumed by the door, hands on hips.

"Move! Get her feet down! This is cruel! The baby will never come out like this!"

The man closed his eyes, unhooked his listening circle from his ear, and folded his arms.

"You must let go of me," said Dylan to the queen. "I have to fix your feet." He twisted one arm free of her grasp, then the other, then—"It'll be all right; you'll feel so much better"—he freed the first arm again. He pulled the woodbox up to the end of the table and stood on it to work out how the shackles were fastened.

"There," he said when the first was undone. He caught the queen's foot and lowered it, hanging on to the open shackle with his other hand as the weight of her other leg dragged it high. She rolled onto her side and curled up tight around her big belly, panting.

Dylan unfastened the second shackle, then clipped the two together. That would be perfect. She could hold on to that.

He climbed down and went to the queen's head. "You'll have to sit up," he said. She opened her eyes and glared at him. "You'll have to." He tried to show her with gestures.

"I've never seen anything like it," the manservant said disgustedly through his talking loop.

Dylan waved him over. "Quick, help me get her up before the next pain comes."

But the servant wouldn't help. The queen, though, was stronger than other birthing mothers Dylan had seen. With only a little help she raised herself halfway to sitting. Then she stopped and laid a hand on her belly, which began to gather itself with the next contraction. An expression of deep astonishment transformed her face.

"Here, grab the chain! Put your feet here on the box!" He helped her place them.

She braced her legs, clung to the chain, and swung forward off the table edge with the contraction. She cried out—*a good, long, pushing cry, that one,* Dylan heard Mum say with a smile. By the light of the odd little lamps dotted around the hut, Dylan saw the bulge of the baby's head top between the queen's thighs. She opened there, a wedge of the head skin showed, scrawled with flat, wet, dark hair—and the contraction was over, and she hung from the chain exclaiming down at him. She was excited now—now that she wasn't strapped down and being tortured.

"I can see it. It's good!" Dylan grinned up at her and kept his hands underneath her to show he was ready to catch the baby. "Now you must do little breaths," he said, "so it doesn't rush out and tear you." *Because if you need stitches, things could get complicated, doctors and hospitals and such. Police, maybe. Immigration people.* "So huh, huh, huh—"

She echoed him. Another contraction came, and her face stretched, but she stayed with him, and the baby's head was out.

The bear pushed forward, vast and grass-smelly at Dylan's shoulder, and licked the top of the baby's head.

"Stop that!" He smacked the black nose and tried to

shoulder the great head away without moving his hands from under the baby. The bear let itself be pushed but swung straight back, snuffing at the baby.

"You there!" he called out to the manservant, trying to push his body in between the bear and the queen's trembling, sweat-slicked thigh. "Grab the honey!"

"I see no honey urn." Good, the silly man had put his listener on again. "I see no urns at all."

"On the shelf, with all the other glass jars. The one with the yellow label." Would he know what *glass* was? Would he know what a *label* was?

The bear was busy behind Dylan. Any old second it would slash open his back with its claws or simply toss him aside. The queen's belly tightened, and her eyes needed him to be there and breathing with her.

"This one?" The servant thrust the jar in front of his face.

Without taking his eyes from the baby, all the time panting with the queen, Dylan grabbed the jar, opened it, put it behind him on the floor, and brought his hand back in time to catch the baby as its shoulders eased out. The rest of the body rushed after it, looped about with the cord, and Dylan had to snatch the baby out of the way as the great crimson cloak of the placenta slithered out as well and fell onto the woodbox.

He checked that the baby was breathing all right, that its mouth was clear. "Here, hold this," he said to the servant over the furry hummock of the bear's back. "No, fetch me a cloth first, from—where is it? From that bag there. Bring the whole bag."

The manservant did so, weeping and exclaiming joyfully.

He took the baby and Dylan passed him one of the ratty, soft old holiday bath towels to wrap it in. Then, working around the bear, which was licking up the spilled honey and exploring the jar with a large, thorough tongue, Dylan folded another towel into a soft pad, put it on the table, and helped the queen lower herself shakily onto it.

He felt Mum's queenly calm inside himself; he knew what to do, and how to move without hurry or stress from one task to the next. He brought Edwin's baby blanket to cover the queen's lap with, and put another towel around her shoulders. He brought her water and she drank thirstily. He brought a bag clamp and a chopping board and Mum's best sharp knife, and attended to the cord.

All the while the manservant crooned. When the umbilical cord was cut and clamped, he handed the baby into the queen's arms. "My lady."

Dylan tidied the placenta into the empty kindling bucket. He put another towel down to soak up the placenta blood on the woodbox. Then he came to the queen's elbow to see the baby. "Oh, it's a girl," he said.

The manservant fumbled his translator to his mouth. "A *princess*. One day to be a *queen*."

"Does she have a name?"

The servant recited a lengthy sentence that the translator could do nothing with. "However," he added, "you will choose a different name for her to use in this place, to keep her safe here, and undiscovered. Something very plain and common."

"To keep her safe here?" said Dylan.

"My lady can hardly take her into battle." The servant rolled his eyes. "You must keep her here until such time as we have cleared the Pestilence and reestablished order."

"We must?"

"Yes, and then we will send for her."

The queen was kissing the baby, its face, its tummy, its protesting legs and arms. She laughed at its squeaking cry and gave a squeaking cry herself. Then she wrapped the baby up and thrust it at Dylan, smiling.

"Um, how long is that likely to be?" he asked the servant. "A week? Two weeks?"

The servant tapped his earpiece and gave a supercilious laugh. "A great deal longer than that," he said.

"Years?"

"Yes, some years, probably."

Years? Dylan knew that this was crazy and impossible; he knew also, in his calm, that there was no point protesting. This was a queen, for goodness' sake! When a queen—a queen with a belt full of knives—tells you to do something, you don't fuss and whinge. You do it or you probably die.

The queen was dressing, visibly gathering strength as she did. Dylan watched her intently. Every layer she put on, all the gray underthings with their ties and drawstrings and monograms, the padded gear to protect the royal skin from the rub of the armor, the armor itself, the broad belt with its stones and scars and heavy sheathed weapons—he memorized it all so he could tell baby . . . baby Jane about it when she grew old enough to understand. He would borrow Uncle Brett's sketchbook tomorrow and try to draw everything, and describe the bits he couldn't draw, like that belly piece the queen was adjusting, now that her belly wasn't so firm and high and full of baby.

The bear idly wandered around the hut. It huffed into corners, drank noisily from the dog's bowl by the door, hoisted itself to its full height to paw things off the mantel.

The manservant went about gathering all the lamps. They were like little glowing crabs propped on their claw tips. They looked delicate, but they must be strong, the way he blew them out and tossed them casually into a bag.

"Very well," he said when only one lamp, on the table, was left. "We must depart. My queen requests that you accept this contribution to the princess's upkeep." He laid a small black pouch on the table.

"Would you please thank Her Majesty—" Mum's calm suddenly drained out of Dylan, and he felt rushed and confused. "For—for this honor."

The servant conveyed his meaning. The queen looked up from adjusting her sword belt. Under her raised faceplate, her eyes brightened with laughter. She strode to Dylan, clapped his head in her jingling, gauntleted hands, and planted on his forehead a kiss that was more metal than flesh. Then she lowered her splendid helmed head to her sleeping daughter and drew in a long breath, as though she would gather in all the baby-scented air around the tiny body. She spoke, and the manservant lifted the last crab lamp to his lips.

There was a stunning snap as he blew it out.

"Oh!" Dylan staggered. Against the complete darkness an

16

afterimage faded from his eyes, of the queen wading back to her world through a knee-high mass of gape-jawed creatures, spiny-eyed, starven-bodied, frozen mid-screech in the flash of other-world light.

"Jibber-jabbers!" Dylan clutched baby Jane to his thudding chest and pressed her cheek to his. She was hot and velvety; she smelled of clean blood and the insides of her mother. She was real. Jibber-jabbers were real, too, but they were somewhere else, closed off from him now, while this soft, harmless baby was here, drawing the pain out of his welted cheek, smoothing the welts flat by contact with her freshness and her newness. The windows and door emerged from the dark, full of motionless, starlit trees. The died-down fire ticked in the stove.

Holding Jane close to keep from shaking too badly, Dylan fetched his torch from among the splinters that had been the head of his bed. He found the figures on the floor, the queen and the manservant by the table, the bear near the stove; he laid them next to the payment pouch on the table. He brought the one unsmashed lamp from the mantel and lit it with a wobbly match struck from an unsteady matchbox. He arranged Jane more firmly in his arms and looked about helplessly. Such a mess! Where to start?

A cry came from outside, from down near the creek—a woman's cry. It was Ella, Ella in labor, Ella about to drop. And Mum, her smiling voice: "That's my girl. Let's have a good push with the next one."

"That's what we'll do," said Dylan. "We'll boil some water." He laid Jane in a nest of clean towels on the table, kissed her frowning forehead, and went to the tank tap. "You always need boiling water when a baby's coming."

The water rushed into the kettle with a nice, normal sound. The princess lay quiet among her cloths, moving her hands slowly as if through water, looking at the rafters with her clouded eyes, breathing in the warmth of the new world.

Monkey's Paternoster

Our Hannimanni was sick. We were all jumpy as fleas.

He sat on the watch rock at the top of the House, at the top of the world, and I would hardly have known of His sickness, except the tremble that went through Him now and again. He kept up the patrols, but they were shorter, and crankier; everywhere He went, He scared a spray of sons and daughters before Him—sometimes even a wife was run off with a claw line in her flank.

"Enough days of this," said Broketooth, my gran-mammy, "and we'll have bachelors at our borders."

"You reckon?" said some cousin, clutching her new child close. "Won't He rally?"

"He might," said Broketooth. She fingered her tooth, which

was full of gray lines, and which her gum was all pouched around, red. "He might not, and then things will be different."

The cousin watched Him snarling and skrarling around down there. "I hope He does get better, and soon."

"Hope away," said Broketooth.

I was pretty small, and I didn't know nothing about Life yet, so I didn't say nothing either way.

Hannimanni came back up. I waited until He had settled, until plenty of others had moved up and shown it was all right to pick at Him, before I went near. I sorted through some of His fur well back behind, where plenty of others would cop it first if He took it in mind to slash out.

He smelled all wrong. I nearly said so to the wife next to me, it was so strong: *How can He smell this bad and still He walks around?* I nearly asked.

Then our servants called us, which I was relieved for, and we bounded down the rocks and along the flats and ridges for our food. They had cakes as well as rooties and fruits of all flavors. I ate and ate in good health; I bulged at the belly.

When I came back, starting to feel sleepy-ful and carrying extra cakes, I met Hannimanni, coming down, but not able to move fast.

"Here," I said, and I gave Him a cake.

"That's good," He said. He did not lift His face to me, nor did He smell, either of sex or anger. He sat and ate, but slowly, as if the cake were poor and He was thinking He might throw it away. I put down my other cakes and rooties and did some part-and-seek among His fur.

21

"That's kind," He said, and ate more, but still without relish.

I felt like I gleamed with health beside Him. It made me bold. "You want to buck up," I said to Him.

"You're right," He said. "I do want to."

"You're all the protection we've got."

I was just mouthing. Protection against what? I'd never come up against more than one of those raggedy doglets, myself. Bachelors, says Broketooth, but those skinny losers? They never come close enough to smell.

"Ay," said Hannimanni, and sighed. "There's such a lot of you. So many sons and gran-sons and gran-dotties. I don't know." He sighed again, and some of it blew at me, smelling of cake and illness.

As we settled that evening in the overhang, some mam said, "I don't like to lie down, somehow. I don't like to close my eyes, this night."

"I wish night would not come," said another.

I thought Broketooth would say *Wish away* at them, but she was busy eyeing very hard all the borders she could see.

I pushed in among those close to her, among their warmths. I watched the sky where the sun had gone, and tried with my eyes to stop the rest of the light from dropping away, too.

What woke me was—well, no one was exactly sleeping. But a bachelor made a wrong leap somewhere close, and shrieked as he died on some wires, and his fellows shrieked, too. They're not very healthy or limber, and they just don't know their way around, here near House Hill. And of course they're always nervous. They know about our Hannimanni's heroic deeds and defenses; if they don't wear a scar themselves, they've got all the legends to make them clumsy.

Anyway, I saw the sparks shower from a pole head, and the bachelor flew all limp and wrong from the wires, then dropped out of sight.

"Oop," said Broketooth. "That one's not going to make Hannimanni."

"Make Hannimanni *what?*" said Kinnick-Tiddit, an older cousin of mine.

"*Become* Hannimanni," said Broketooth. "Make us a new Hannimanni, of himself. Take over. He weren't big enough anyway. Lands, my tooth hurts, this early. Come up, sun."

A new Hannimanni? What was she talking about?

"Take over?" said Kinnick-Tiddit.

"Well, look at Our Father," said Broketooth.

Several of us came out of the overhang and did so. There He was, flat along Top Ledge.

"He looks dead already. Paw Him, someone. Go up there."

"You go. You paw Him."

"No, you. I've got this babby. Go on. He should be up and running about. Look, everywhere, they're popping up, those smellies."

A growl bubbled inside Hannimanni, but there was no gleam of eyes. Every other head of us, though, the eyes were opening—*plink* here, *plink* there, mammies and babbies alike. Heads were popping up all about, look-look, foreheads wrinkling. On every rock and ledge the piles of us were clamming

23

together tighter, while all around our borders loser-heads bobbed up, bobbed down, bobbed up somewhere else.

I sat in the middle of a pile; all the bobbing, all the looking about, made me feel chittery. I had to chew on an old, not-very-choice piece of sweet-rooty to stop myself bursting out of the clammed pile and running—running anywhere, anywhere there wasn't a bachelor bobbing up, right in front of me, which wasn't smart, with so many of them about.

Everyone was getting to the same state. The ones with the babs was worst, crooning and twitching and trying to talk away their fear.

"If we were to go right up on the top of the House," said someone, "right up onto the lap of that carvenservant, onto its head, maybe a ring of our teeth would keep them back, keep them off us."

"Yeah," said Broketooth nastily. "Or maybe if we grew wings. Or maybe if we just now grew twice as big as we are, with twice as long teeth."

"There's got to be some way," whimpered a mammy.

Broketooth just sucked on her tooth. Everyone would have preferred to hear her scoff more, but she didn't.

The bachelors were getting bolder, particularly as the center of us was deadish-gray Hannimanni lying there, instead of the explosion of danger that He usually was. Any moment now, I thought, He will bound up and start priding around and snapping His lips back, going big at these smelly boys, pissing on everything, making the world smell right again. Any moment.

But He continued to lie. His eyes, among all our fearful

ones, were idle, soft in the firstening light, as if this were a day of leisure just dawning, not of battle. I swallowed a hard piece of rooty and chewed off another.

A loser, a big one—I didn't know they grew so big in the wild!—he danced right up the House and paused by Top Ledge. Then he came forward to sniff the situation of our Hannimanni.

"Insolence!" chattered a frightened mam.

"You *stink*!" shouted another at the line of bachelors creeping toward us. Everyone at the edge drew in their tails, and some showed teeth at them.

The big one leaned right in close to Hannimanni, who lay there drowsy, showing the very tips of His teeth, His lip too languorous to roll back and cover them.

On a House ledge across from us, a pile of wives blew apart. I heard the scutter and the screaming, but I didn't look. I was busy—we were all busy—watching these dancers mince forward, shrink back, try different roundabout ways at us. Bachelor heads hung out from the stone above, whiskers against the sky; they were there at the edge of my eye just as the fleeing mammies and children were there, even while I was fixed, all of me, on the biggest, nearest dancer as he propped and sneaked toward the overhang.

I could see everything, smell all the smells; everything was still. Even this bachelor was still, for the moment, because Broketooth had snarled. I smelled the sparky smell from the wires, and the poor-food funk of bachelor, and the sweetness of morning garden; the last star faded with a smell just like a drop of water drying off sunny carvenstone.

Then they jumped in among us.

"Never!" someone screamed.

We ran—except we weren't *we* anymore. Each was a lone dottie, without help or hero, a tiny sole vulnerable, running across the rocks, bounding up among the carvens, smelly shadows at her tail. I seen one of those paws dash a little babby head to the rock, like breaking an egg. I turned and seen that mother taking it, all teeth and trembling, the bloke behind her keeping her in place with his claws, working at her all intent. They're everywhere, the filth, the gray filth, each sprouting a sex that's the first proper color of the day. They bound and they look and they follow and we can't be not seen, none of us can. Here's one and another, finishing off, pulling out, running after.

"Hannimanni, save us!" is calling my auntie and one of my sisters as we run.

I save my breath, but it makes no difference. In the middle of my skitter one of them is on me, smacking me down, knocking out my breath. He takes me in his claws and he shafts me; he breaks open the back of me and forces himself right up inside me, all the way up through to my gaping head. It doesn't take long to bang and pump me full of pain, full of his stink of wild rocks and untapped water, and the breath you get when all you eat is thorn bushes.

Then he stops and is gone, and all the losers have run on, and I'm dropped like a bit of cake crust, or a rooty end that's chucked aside for fresher food. Except I hurt; I lie on the rock and I hurt; I lie still so as not to hurt worse.

Kinnick-Tiddit sits nearby and shivers. She makes the rock wet with her sitting. She's holding someone's bab, that's chewed and dying. The fight is moved out from us all around, a ruff of noise at the edges, like the pale fur around a face.

Kinnick-Tiddit hovers her nostrils over the torn parts of the bab. "This one have had the gong; that bachelor have killed it, the rough bugger."

I can't speak yet; I'm not yet returned from the wild. The pain is all up inside and around me like a stinging mud. I sit in it and be surprised, closed-eyed and tremoring just like Hannimanni yesterday.

They're chasing Him off.

"Byaa!" they shout in the distance. "Go and feast your fat face on slave garbage!"

"Aye! Donkey dung! Try that!"

"Moldy cake crusts! See how you do!"

Closer is Broketooth's voice, queered in such a way that I know she have took it, too: "Don't you come to me bleeding and weeping. Don't you go thinking Our Father behaved any different when He came to us."

And around her whimper all the mothers torn of children, all the dotties hollowed out behind.

Our servants came, but just to look; they had no food. They found the dead bachelor below us. The stupids, they gathered him onto a cloth just as if he were a proper creature; they covered him with powders and flowers and carried him off for veneration—when there were all these babbies, some on the rock and stone like rubbished fruit skins, some still in the arms of mams and cousins, staining and mystifying them.

They tidied them away eventually. By then the babbies

smelled bad, and had all been laid down by their mams. The first big mams were climbing the watch rock and the new Hannimanni was letting them come at Him and groom. My pain was pretty much gone by then, and I was clearing in my head about it all.

The funk of wildness is fading from the new man's smell. He's beginning to be right for us, essential, handsome. Little fights are breaking out all the time, mild better-'n-you fights; I myself have bested old Drumbreast, who was a touch too big for me before.

I sit at the edge. The new Hannimanni struts here and there, chasing off any bachelors that still hang around, clawing up a girlfriend as His fancy takes Him. I keep well away from Him yet.

Food! Food is the thing now. From here I reckon I can smell the fruits being chopped in our servants' houses. I can hear the juice drip to board and floor, and the breads and cakes swelling in their cookers. The sawing of knife through rooty is like an itch all over me. Our servants bring us broad platters crowded with colored smells. We run to meet them, farther from the House than I've ever been.

All us dotties, we're all running, we're all grabbing more than we can hold, we're all eating like mad, each enough for two.

A Good Heart

I loved Annie Stork and she loved me. We never done the dancy-dancy, but I most certainly thought we would end up wed. I were looking babies into that girl's eyes, even if I weren't putting them into her below.

So smack yourself, Arlen Michaels, smack yourself in the head and get out of this bush and away from here. What do you want to cause yourself such pain for? *You ought try always*, don't Nanna say, *to add to the tally of happinesses in the world and good works, in everything you do. You ought be trying for no one's harm.*

Well, I aren't. No one's harm at all. Or at least no one's but my own, and what should that matter?

Ooh, there sounds the horn, off among the trees. Soon they'll be here, and I won't have the choice to run off. I dither, bunching my shirt neck with my nervous hands. The white ribands loll down from the trees all round the clearing. How can I bear to walk away from them? How can I bear to stay? All those small evidences of the Lord-son's riches are like this, like watching Baker Marten pull from his oven some vast cake I will never get a piece of.

Now it's voices. Some of them still sing the song that swept the happy pair out of town. Some call and laugh over the music. The footfalls of the two horses thud uneven and slow through the whole hill. Now it is too late; now I must stay put or I'll be seen. Fool. Knothead. What are you doing, hiding, peeping, like Dotty Cinders through women's winders? Why aren't you off fishing or dogging or being of some useful help to someone?

There's movement, the color on something, the Lord-son's sleeve, maybe, or that cloth around the horse that is like a broidered tent. Hup, here they come.

The leaves wag in front of my face, in front of my great sad sigh. Here come the two splendid lord's beasts in their tents, and borne upon their backs the Lord-son in his robes and Annie Stork in her bride raiment, oh my gracious, white as a waterfall and with that yellow cloak over all, stiff with gold-thread embroidery. Don't know why you're so surprised, Arlen. You saw all this down in the square before you took flight up here. Don't know why your heart is choosing *now* to split, tube from chamber, and all your blood pour out the opening.

The servants help the bride down. The picture comes to me of Annie when she were little, sitting on her step, her white-aproned lap full of pine seeds; she were pinching the skins off them one by one like you do, chattering like she'd never stop. She's another creature now, in that dress and bearing. She'll never be back on her step and simply dressed, shining with her own beauty alone and unbejeweled. Likely I'll never speak to her again, or she to me except as a high to a lowling, thanking me for some service—holding the gate, maybe, for her to pass through on a grand horse such as this, for they have plenty of horses, the Lord and his son. Likely she'll call me *Mister Michaels* then, not *Arlen*, not *you great puddin-head* as she did when I tickled her that time, not *darlin* as she said once, very low and growly and daring, and quite near her parents' ears.

Now they have all sailed into the clearing like ships into harbor, the whole party. Horses are tethered, cloths are spread, baskets are swung down from shoulders. The clean faces of the high house, with their ornamental collars below and their head-wears above, laugh and smile and look about with pleasure. "What a lovely setting!" says one of the ladies, and everyone agrees: "Lovely. Lovely."

I'm an only son, I said to my friend Tater, sticking my chin out.

Uh-huh? He peered at me as if he couldn't believe me. *So?*

So I'll come into the house, one day. I'll come into that little bit of land, and whatever stock—

Tater went weak at the knees with laughing. He leaned against the front of the Eel and Basket and shook. I looked very frosty at him, but he only laughed even harder.

Eventually he knew better than to laugh on, or I would have thumped him. *But your gramp's got to die first*, he spluttered. *And then your dad! And even then, she'd have to share with that fierce ould nanna of yours and that mother! That mother! I'd be looking to share a rolling barrel with ten pound of sharp rocks before I'd move into your house with that tongue and those eyes!*

Truly I never thought the thing so hopeless until he said that. That's how far a girl's smile and a girl's shape can bend the world for you.

But she did love me; she said so! *You're a fine man, Arlen Michaels*, she said out back of the Eel at Midsummer, and she'd had only a little ale. *And you've a good heart*. I can still feel her finger, poking me in the chest—that finger there with its rings, that hand in its Lord's hand, the lace cuff resting across the knuckles in the sunshine.

Those lips so graciously smiling now, I can still feel their kiss on my mouth. I floated home that Midsummer Eve, tipping the fieldwalls and the treetops with my toes. The future ran out ahead of me like a carpet roll kicked open down the town hall steps. Kisses, wedding, children; step, step, step. And on all sides, people clapping me on the back, people smiling—yes, even my mam. One touch of Annie Stork's lips and everything remade itself around me full of hope and sweetness.

But then, as I'm waiting for my next chance for kisses—still floating a little from the first one, even, still surviving on that—Mam brings the news home, don't she, of Lord Gowper's son returning from his uncle's, of that launderer's girl Annie Stork catching his eye.

She's pretty enough, said Nanna. *You can see why she would.*

Mam shafted me with one of her side glances, where I sat by

the door, blown from a day's ditchdigging for Parson Hubble and with my face already burning from what she'd said. *Been saving herself for some such, that one. Always thought herself above the wash.*

Too good to slap and scrub, eh? said Nan with a cackle.

Unless a lord's soft hand is doing the slapping, it seems.

They've done with eating, now. The lutenist is picking out something slow, and some of them are drooping and sliding to their cushions. Annie Stork isn't among the droopers. She's upright and thoughtful, as if she must keep watch on all the happenings, to make sure they don't tatter into dreams and she find herself in her gray smock again, a lone laundry maid sitting in an empty clearing.

"Rest awhile, my love," says her new husband, touching her gleaming sleeve.

"No, I must . . . go into the forest," she says with her new accent all clear and cool, and a modesty that no other laundress in the town would show.

"Who can accompany you?" he says, half sitting up.

"No, no," she says. "I'll not go far."

And up she gets and comes straight for me! She's seen me, my great eyes, she's *felt* me staring all through the picnic and the entertainments, she's out to tear me from the bush here and shame me and send me away! Or worse, she'll make her toilet behind this very bush, within my sight and hearing, unaware of me. I huddle and freeze and burn while she passes.

She goes, thank God, quite far in among the trees. Not invisibly far—I can still see her head when she stops, before and

34

after she squats, while she bends and turns, arranging her clothing. I can see that when she's done, she glances back toward the clearing, then turns and makes off *away*, farther into the forest.

I come alive all over in that serious way, as when you first see the bunny you're going to have that night for dinner, and your full attention fixes to the back of its neck and tells the rest of you exactly what to do. There was something un-bridely in that glance of Annie's, something serious and certain, something that calculated her chances. I get out of that bush—I swear, without a rustle, I'm so intent—and I follow her.

Quickly she goes, down to the stream. She takes off her embroidered slippers and gathers her cloak and her skirts and underskirts all up and steps sure-footed across the water-glazed stones. Then up the steeper far bank she goes, yellow and white and glittering against its darkness, thin black branches hurrying down across the shape of her. I can't follow her yet; it's too open. Once she tops the slope and goes on, I will come out of the thicket here. I'll go wide, so that if she comes back on a sudden she'll not see me.

But she stops, halfway up the bank. She turns to the left and runs lightly along it, quite far, and I can't follow yet. Then she pauses where the trees thicken, just under a spreading ash there, and she moves about only a little, seeking something.

I am watching her closely. I am straining my eyes and my hunter's skin and my hunter's mind. When she finds what she's after, my shoulders drop, as hers do, with the relief of it. *There you are*, her whole body seems to say. Who is it? I search the forest in front of her, but I can't see no one.

She steps forward. She bends low.

"Milady?"

Annie Stork snaps upright. I jolt like a startled cat myself. It's one of the ladies, calling out from the clearing.

"I'm coming!" Annie calls, her voice all panic and guilt, and she runs back along the slope.

"Do you need assistance?" cries the lady.

"No, no," says Annie from the far side of the stream. "I'm coming back now." Quickly she steps across, and then stamps her feet dry in the grass there, and pushes them into the slippers, and smooths her skirts. Then she pauses, right by my thicket. I drop my gaze so my eyes won't draw hers. She's close enough for me to reach through these leaves and touch the gold thread upon her yellow cloak. I could whisper, and she would hear, and those up above in the clearing would not. I could grasp that white neck and bring her down, so sudden and strong she'd not have time to utter.

As if she heard that thought, Annie puts her white hand with its rings to her collared throat. She looks up toward the clearing and she calms herself, breathing deeply twice, huffing the breaths out. And she sets off up the slope, not hurrying now, step by slow step, a laundress no more.

The blood beats in my head and hands as I watch her go. I don't move until I hear people greet her and scold her up there. Then I'm across the sunlit stream in three quick strides, up the soft dark slope beyond. I follow the trail of her small disturbances in the thick leaf mold along the slope.

When I get there I can't see anything. My hunter's mind has left me, that clearest, cleverest ice drop at the center that knows things without words or doubt. I'm just a boy peering around in a forest, not knowing what to look for. There's no extra movement anywhere, no sound, nothing furtive. Only forest going about its quiet business.

I'm about to bend as Annie did when I see it: a scrap of sacking wedged in a fork of the ash, just above my head. The two rotted ends dangle.

Seeing the sky through their weave, I don't want to look below. My hunter's mind says to me, *Turn and go, while you still can choose. This, you don't want to know.*

Anyone watching would think the air had turned to aspic, is how long it takes me to lower myself. The rest of the cloth is a flat tangle on the forest floor, near invisible. My hand goes out to it snail-slow. The very tips of my fingers catch the edge of the sacking, and lift it through the thickened air, and cast it back.

Underneath is other cloth, finer, paler, with a shape inside. I don't want to touch it. *And you don't have to,* says my hunter's mind. *See? You've a second chance to walk away. Take it, take it. Go.* My breath, through my teeth, sounds like a straw broom sweeping a stone step.

The white cloth is stained and stiff. Its wrinkles stick a little to what's inside, but then come away.

How did I know—because I did know, the way Annie moved, the forest pounding around me, this voice in my head— that I was walking up to a door, that when it opened, what was behind it would knock the head from my shoulders and set it rolling, rolling, all known things turning to flash and shadow before my eyes?

Inside are curled the remains of a tiny, tiny child. Hung in the sacking, high away from the beasts, it died and dried and all smell went out of it, and it fell, this little leather creature. Its skull-face peers out from where ants or some such have nibbled the leather away. Its hands aren't big enough even to grasp the tip of my finger.

And it lay here—how long, how long? There'll be a time to apply myself to that question, but for now, that it lay here *at all* and that I, Arlen Michaels, breathe above it, that I have it in my eyes, is enough and too much for me.

I cover the child with the white cloth, with the sacking, exactly as they were before. When I stand, it's as if *I* were the one as lay stiff dead under the trees all this time; my knees and hips and elbows crack straight, my head is as heavy as rock on my neck, weighted with eyes and thoughts.

Someone else does my walking for me, out of that place, widely around the hill. Take the long way, Arlen, and you'll not meet anyone. "Annie Annie Annie," I whisper like some mad person. It seems the only thing I can say or think, for a while.

I walk out onto Clear Top into all the sky. I stride to the edge and look out over town, that mottle-stone place running with gossip and judgment. My heart beats hard, and Annie's finger prods my chest again. *You've a good heart,* she says. Prod, she goes, prod-prod. How I glowed at that girl's touching me! But now I see: a good heart's not that daffy grinning, floating away fresh-kissed across the fields; it isn't that chestful of passion you bring to her prettiness, all full and flaming.

A good heart is when a girl that you loved, a girl who has

pained you and chosen another in your stead—chosen two others!—places in your hands this precious and dreadful thing, the means to her own ruin. And you could tell it abroad, and everyone you know, from the lads up to your own mam and dad, would say you were right to tell, would nod and shake your hand and say, *That Lord-son should know what kind of a wife he's got him,* and you could shine all bright and right in their outrage, glamorous in your injuries and your lost love. But you keep silent, because you can do that, too, and a *good heart* would do that, a *fine man,* a man who truly loved Annie Stork.

You saw her serious face in the forest, her strong feet wet upon the green-golden river stones. You saw her white hand calming the breath in her throat. Let her be lucky now; let her be a lady; have pity.

My heart's not pounding no more. It sits instead like a big hard bruise in my chest, paining green in the middle, frilling blood-purple round the edge. It takes a lot of carrying, to get it to the pathway, to keep it moving down the hill in the sunlight. I need my mam; I need her to snap at me and order me about; I need her to shrink this day to something Michaels-sized, that doesn't hurt so hard and weigh so heavy.

I round the bend. Top Gate stands open and I start to run. I run right through the town and out the other side. All the way down to Lower Feld I go. I slide to a stop at our place, and sit on the step panting, collecting myself, readying myself to go in.

Winkie

Ollyn lay awake among the snoring Keller kids. The man goggled in at her through the window.

I will go home, she thought. Somehow. As soon as he's gone. I will run out of here; I will run home. No matter about the new baby coming; I will sit quiet in a corner. Only, I can't be here. I can't be here a moment longer than I have to be. I am just not brave enough.

"Skinny little thing, aincha?" Tod Keller had said when she sidled in their kitchen door last evening. "I never even noticed you among those roustyboys, your brothers."

Ma Keller had laughed, a sudden laugh that made Oll start. "Tuck her away in the press," she said. "Pop her on the mantel for the night, couldn't we, petal?" Her finger under Oll's chin had scraped like splintery wood.

He was too tall a man. He was extraordinarily tall. No one else she knew could look in over the sill of an upstairs window. If it could be called looking when a person's eyes swivvered left and right like that, never meeting up in the same direction—at least as far as Oll had seen. She'd had the good sense, when an eye-beam swung near, to lie limp and asleep-looking. She breathed slowly while her heart banged like a soldiers' band.

He shifted out there in the laneway, and muttered some question to himself. He rapped softly on the windowpane, and it was all Oll could do to not cringe at the sound, which was spongy somehow, as well as bony.

Go away, you horror, she thought, so I can get home from here.

Ple-ease! Why was she like this? She knew her ma hated it, and yet the whining came up from her deeps and she needed, needed to be pressed up against warm Ma; couldn't see why Ma would not stop a moment what she was doing and hold on to her and make things all right. Just the once would do.

Get her off me, Ma had said through her teeth.

Huvvy had peeled her off claw by claw. *Come here, you little limpet, you little sticky octopoddle*, he laughed as she wailed.

Ollyn had lost her head a moment, thinking she would die of her distress.

And that was when Ma had rounded on her. *It's because of this you must go, silly girl! All this clinging and sooking, you're sending me mad!*

Ollyn had blinked silent at Ma's vehemence; Huvvy had stopped laughing and held her quite firm and protectingly.

43

But Ma had kept on. *Our baby will not come out with you around! It will not want to see the face that horrible noise comes out of!*

She was bent over them; Huvvy and Oll were blown back by the wind of her anger. They all three had leaned like that a moment.

Take her, Huv. Take her to Kellers'. I can't stand it any longer. And Ma had turned away and spread her hands on the table and gritted her teeth there with a pain.

Get your nightgown, Huvvy had murmured in Oll's ear, and she had hurried to do so.

The man's feet, on the cobbles, slid, paused, and then slapped. His muttering moved away from the window. Oll waited, because her heart of hearts knew he might well come back to a window he had peered in before. But she could not wait too long, because she must see which direction he went in, so she could avoid him.

Up she got from between fat Anya and bony Sarra Keller, and ran lightly to the window, keeping to the shadows. She pressed her cheek to the window frame.

At first she didn't see him up the lane. Oh, she thought, maybe I only dreamed him. But I will go home anyway. Ma will protect me from my dreams.

But then a clot of shadow moved low against that door, at the top of those stairs there, and a high cry snaked down the lane, and the thing, the man, unfolded himself, the full kinked lanky height of him, with his shining round head, a few hairs streaked across it, a few others floating out sideways, bright and frizzly in the lamplight.

Watching him crane to see into that house, hearing his cry, Oll was like Mixie Dixon's doll that her pa brought from Germany, held together with stiff wires. How will I *get* home, she thought, if I cannot even move?

The man's nightgown confused her eye. It was made of the oddest-shaped patches, all patterned differently. Buttons gleamed here and there. Unhemmed, it stroked his stringy calves with fraying threads. His feet—look how many cobbles his feet covered! Oll was likely to faint with it.

He swayed out from the window, back toward the Kellers', and called, in a high, reasonable voice borrowed from someone sane, someone real, "*Well* past! *So* far past their bedtime!" Then he loped up the steps past Draper Downs's house, where there were no children, and past the House of the Indigent Aged. And around into Spire Street, to the *right*, turning *up* the hill.

Oll's wires turned to workable muscle again, and her mind cleared somewhat. Ma, she thought. Ma. She must put herself near Ma.

She did not dress. She did not take her clothes. She did not even stop for boots. In her nightdress, cool air puffing inside it, she ran noiselessly down the stairs.

The cat by the coals lifted its black head as she passed. The kitchen door was just like the one at home; she knew how to raise the latch, hold it up while she tiptoed through, and lower it silently behind her.

It was a clear, cold night, the sky thick-frosted with stars. A part of Oll quailed and quaked and covered its head inside her, while her body ran stiffly along the house path, across the back of Kellers' and down the narrow side way. She peeped around into the lane, and there was the same view as from the upper room, the fine-cut keystone over Draper Downs's door, the House's curly iron sign silhouetted against the lamplit wall—except she was lower in this view now, so much more at the mercy of things, and the night was cold, cold.

She dived down into the shadows to her left, stubbing her toe on a cobble but not stopping, not even missing a step to hop. She gasped out the pain as she ran. Her breath was the only sound, that and the slight rubbings and shiftings of her nightgown, which was soft and damp with sleep, chilling around her. Her feet made no sound on the cobbles, their soles being smooth and damp, too, and Oll being so light. The row houses of Pitcher Street flew past her up the hill.

A noise in the square, just before she reached it, made her slide to a stop; her hair swung out, and her nightdress hem, just to the house corner exactly and no farther. The clank of the lamplighter's hook, the squeak of the lamp door. The scrape of the lamplighter's boots. His sweetish pipe smoke wisped around the corner and tickled her nose.

She ran back up Pitcher Street; it was far to the first lane. She hid and, panting, peeped back down. There: he was crossing the end of the street, attending to the lamp, closing it—and moving on around the square?

No. Oll swallowed a whimper. The lamplighter was coming up Pitcher Street. She could go to him, perhaps; she could ask him to take her home. He would have to.

But I'm not brave enough, she thought. I can't go up and talk to a man, not in the middle of the night, not after seeing that other. And she ran away along the lane.

She could have taken the back way behind the row houses, but a dog was barking somewhere down there, and the noise was too much for her all by itself in this huge night. So she ran on to Swale Street—and out into the middle of the street she ran, and down she ran in the full lamplight right alongside the drain there, so that when the tall patched shadow unkinked itself from a doorway uphill, why, there she was, clear as anything, little and live as he could wish for.

"Ooh, there's one!"

She skittered aside like a rat, under a jettied upper floor. There was nowhere to run on to, though; however much she searched, and however small she was, no cavity could hide her.

His great feet walked down Swale Street, treading with exaggerated care. His voice fluted up there among the stars. His nightgown—Oll was the wired-together doll again. His gown was made of many nightdresses, she saw now, small ones, unpicked, spread flat, and clumsily sewn together.

His knees came down inside the nightgown cloth like two great tree bolls falling from a woodcutter's cart, and his fists came down like two more, either side of the jutting room.

Ollyn wilted and whimpered and shrank into a ball.

His face came down: his wide mouth with bad teeth saying, "Where can she be, my little mousette?" in that too-high voice; his nose, long and uneven and gristly-looking, with sprays of dark hairs from the nostrils; and eyes, so big and so mismatched, searching, searching, first this one, then that.

"Ah. Ha-ha-*ha*." That was his own voice, that deep one, that rougher one. "But you can't make yourself small *enough*, can you?"

She looked from eye to eye. *Ma,* she mouthed, and tears came.

"That's what I like to see," he said.

He picked her up and brought her out and examined her, laying her flat across the palms of his big hands. She could not identify the bad smell of them.

And then she was too busy trying to breathe, because he had stopped her mouth with soft wax, tied it in with a rag. She was near dead with fright, just as a mouse or bird will die in your hand, from being so enclosed.

He held her tight and carried her out of town the misty, marshy way, the way no one walked—but then, no one had such long legs as these; he gathered up his patchwork night-gown and stepped across the marsh's lumps and glimmers. Her feet swung out in the cold like bell clappers, but struck noise from nothing. The man waded in among trees, where it was still misty, and then onto drier ground. He put Oll down and pinned her with his foot while he lifted a door in the side of a mound of earth. He carried her inside, and the door closed and entombed them.

Dizzy, her eyes full of stars that weren't there, no voice to scream with and no breath to cry, Ollyn stayed limp where he had laid her, on wood as scratchy as Ma Keller's fingers. Her eyelids turned dimly red as he made a light. Such a smell! He frightened her eyes open, speaking close. "Let's look at you." He was there with a smutchy lamp. She was on a table, and he sat down by it. The dark parts of his eyes skated about on his eyeballs. He propped her upright, took a tool, cut through the rag around her mouth, and hooked the wax out. "There," he said. "Squeak to me. Squeak as loud as you like."

When she did not, he poked her in the tum. "Blink, then. Show me how you can blink."

This she did, and it delighted him. His delight was all brown teeth and spittle and spongy hands clapping.

Oll blinked some more; blinking was better than being eaten.

"Yes, that'll do." He smacked her so that she fell sideways on the table. "No need to be a smarty-britches."

He brought his face close to hers, pointed to his own staring eyes with his flat fingers. "You see these?"

She nodded, still dazed from the blows.

"Do you see blinkers? Do you see any lids?"

Ollyn shook her head.

"You know what my name is, by those that rule the world, those mums and das, those butchers and merchants and clerks and councilors?"

She shook her head again. Maybe if she did not utter, he would not harm her.

"Wee Will Winkie. 'Wee' because I am so *big*, you see. 'Winkie' because I *cannot* wink. I cannot wink, or blink, or sleep. I can barely *see* for my dry eyes and their irritations; do you see how red are these eyes?"

Oll nodded.

"I will show you," he said. He darted away, darted back. "Cannot wink, or blink, but *aahh*, he can think, this one. And you shall help me."

He went off and rummaged in the shadows. "I have hid them, in case of intruders," he said in a muffled voice. "Beasts, you know, or thieves."

The lamplight did not push back much of the darkness. Boxes, she thought, were stacked in a corner. There was a heap of cloths, another heap of scrambled dark shapes—firewood, perhaps, from some twisty kind of tree. A fire snoozed in a filthy, rusted stove; the rotten smell near smothered her.

"Here." Out of the corner the giant came. He placed— either side of the lamp so that they lit up like lamps themselves— two large finger-smudged flasks made of glass. They were nearly full with clear water. The rocking stirred the fine white sediment on the bottom, which spiraled up slowly. In each flask something like a mottled pig's ear hung from gray threads that passed up through a wax-sealed hole in the flask's broad cork and trailed off across the table.

"Aren't they beautiful?" said the giant. "So much work in them."

Ollyn examined one pink-and-brown glowing shape. The work was—

"Stitches," she said, surprised into speech. It was clumsy stitches.

"Yes!" he said. "Stitches-stitches, in the softest skin! *Many* nights' work. And look along the bottom—what do you see there?"

"Uh . . . a—a *fringe*." A fringe of tiny spikes. Of hairs.

"Of real lashes." He breathed the words into her face. "Of *real* lashes! Can you believe it?"

"It's. It's. It's." She waved a hand helplessly at the flasks, thinking she might faint, or be sick, from this smell and this sight, the fleshy patchworks hanging, glowing. She looked away, but the only other thing to see besides the giant's face was his nightgown, which had so much the same appearance, the different colors, the seams, the shapes of arms and chests, but splayed out, spread out as if flayed from—

"I want my ma," she said to him, trying not to boo-hoo it, trying to speak as if she were one giant talking to another. Tears weaseled out of her eyes. "I want Ma and Pa, and Huvvy and Daff and all my brothers. You must let me go home."

He seemed startled, but when she was unable to stifle a hiccup and a teary sniff, he relaxed again. "How about," he singsonged, "a nice hot cup of tea, eh? And a bit of . . . cake. I have a cake."

"I don't want a cake," whispered Oll, but he went looking. She pulled her legs up under her nightgown and wept into her knees as he moved things and dragged things and muttered.

"Was over *here*," he said. "I put the child *here*, 'cause it was broken, and the cake *here*. Although maybe I have mixed that up. Maybe it is among—"

He started to rearrange the pile of twisty firewood. The bad smell was much worse all of a sudden. Oll choked into the cloth of her nightgown, trying to see through her tears.

"Agh," he said. "Well, how about—these is good for a

snack, after they've lain awhile." He looked doubtfully at the pile. He had one in his hand, by its little blackened leg. As Oll watched, the leg came out of its rotten hip socket, and the rest of the baby fell back onto the pile.

The sounds of the breaking, of the falling, stayed in the air a moment.

Then, too fast to think, Oll exploded off the table. She could not be faster than him, but she beat him to the door. She was not strong enough, but she lifted the heavy wooden hatch. She was not very clever, but she ran behind the mound and flattened herself to the grass there, and when Will Winkie burst out of the hatch and stood howling toward the town she clawed a stone out of the ground, and she knelt up and threw it high into the mist, so that it splashed down into marsh water far out in front of him.

The giant plunged after it, still howling. It will not fool him long, Oll thought. He will come back and search here. And she crept down and slipped into the marsh's edge and found a place where she could crouch and rest her head against a hummock, to look like another hummock. It was shockingly cold, that water, but she must hide. And when she was hidden, if she kept very tight and still, wrapping her arms about her bent legs, there was a small amount of warmth that she could harbor there, and her feet and ankles warmed their mud socks just a tadge, and she would not quite die.

She lifted her head. She was in the Kellers' upper room.

"Did you sleep well?" said fat Anya without turning over.

"Yes, thank you," said Ollyn timidly.

But then all the Keller kids got up at once, and their faces were mud, and their nightwear was soaked with it, and they trooped wetly to the stairhead, mud sliding from their hanging fingers, trailing mud behind them on the floor, and they slopped downstairs to Ma Keller, who was frying something and calling them in her fluting voice.

Oll woke under the stars. It was quite warm in the water now. The shivering had stopped. She did not want to move; certainly she did not want to feel that night air on her wet skin. Besides, if she were not carried by a giant, she could not get across the marsh without drowning. She must wait for daylight and find a way, hummock to hummock, somehow.

She opened her eyes. Sparse golden leaves on black branches moved against a blue sky. She was a warm baby, at home, without thoughts or cares. Voices somewhere spoke of everyday matters, quietly so as not to disturb her, without urgency or anger.

Her eyes blinked open. The stars had tilted in the sky. Other lights, midsummer lights, flashed and moved on the marsh water. Voices spoke, the voices from her dream, nothing to be afraid of. She laid her head against the hummock again; perhaps she could sink back into that dream?

They were raising her from the marsh—her corpse, for she was surely dead; she could do nothing with her legs and arms, only feel them hanging off her like quarter sacks of grain.

"He killed me, then," she said.

"What's that, Olliepod?" Huvvy's head was huger than a giant's against the stars.

"She spoke?" said Pa somewhere.

"He threw me on the pile," Oll managed. "He . . . he cut off my eyelids for his jar, for his own."

"Ollie, are you in there?" said Huvvy, frightened. "Is our Ollie in there, or is she bewitched somehow?"

She *did* have eyelids; they drooped across her sight. She was wrapped like a baby in rough, dry cloth. She was shivering, shivering. The shivering shook her whole body and almost all her mind. She was cold against her pa. He was chafing her arm and shoulder back to life through the blanket.

"Did you go into his house?" she said through her shivering jaws. "Did you see all those babies?"

"That house there?" Pa pointed, and she saw the mound fading into the moonlit mist.

"Did *you* cleave it?"

"What's that, my darling?"

"Did you break it like that, the top of it?"

"It were broken all along, Ollyn. It were rotten wrecked when we found it. And no babies inside, loved one. Nothing inside at all but earth. I saw it myself, and Huv and his lamp. Because we looked good and hard in there. Your ma said you might well be in there, buried. But we dug it apart and you weren't. Then and then only, when we were spent and giving up, did you move yourself, and make that cry in the marsh water."

"Like a little cat," said Daff, rowing. "Miou, miou."

"I don't remember," said Oll.

"Of course not," said Huvvy. "You were just about insensible."

Ollyn and Ma scoured the pots, down by the stream. It was Ma's first outing since the baby. They were both numb-fingered with scrubbing, and the wind blew unpredictably, buffeting them off balance and twitching their hair.

"How did you know?" said Oll.

"Know what?" Ma slapped a fresh handful of sand into the rinsed stewpot.

"Where to find me. Where to tell Pa and Huvvy to go that night. And to get a boat. How'd you know about that man?"

Ma scrubbed. "Everyone knows about that man."

"Pa didn't. And 'How'd she get there?' says Huvvy. And I told them and they said, 'Ooh, sounds like Romany Tom' or someone. They would have guessed and guessed, and gone out and had someone thrown in the jail, if you didn't shut them up."

Ma scrubbed on. There was a stubborn set to her.

Well, Oll could be stubborn, too. "So *not* everyone knows." She was back on her heels now, not even pretending to scour. "How'd you know any of it? Pa says you woke him and told him where to go if I weren't at Kellers', where to look. Kellers didn't even know I was gone from bed until he knocked them up."

Ma gave her head a little toss. With the wind, her hair clambered back into her eyes, as busy and black as dueling spiders.

"Ma?"

"What."

"Well?"

Ma lifted the wet sand and let it dribble into a turdy pile in the pot: *blat-blat-blat, blat-blot.* "All my babies," she said. "They wake in the night? I wake. I knew it were you in a minute. The way you carried on about going up to Kellers', I knew you would not stay put."

Oll laughed. "How *could* I wake you, halfway across the town?"

"I don't know." Ma bent to scrubbing again. "There must be a sound you make, your eyelids opening. It carries to my ears."

Oll watched Ma's wayward hair, her determined shoulders, her white-and-purple feet with the toes digging into the sand. These sights satisfied her like a solid meal in her belly. "But what about those other children, the dead ones, on the pile? Does not every mother hear that eyelid sound?"

Ma bunched up her mouth in thought. She rinsed the pot in the stream, holding it out wide where it would catch the clearer, faster water. "I don't know"—she swirled the water in the pot—"how it is for other mothers. I can only say how it is for me."

Through the fiddle and rush of the stream they heard the baby's thin cry. They sat straight to see over the bank, up to the house. Daff was carrying her down, her tiny fists and feet awheel in his awkward arms, her blanket dangling.

"Oh Lord," sighed Ma. "Take her, Ollyn, while I finish here. Wrap her tight and walk her up and down. *Behind* the house, where I can't hear her noise so well."

Oll climbed the bank. The sunlight dazzled her after the

shadowy stream bank; the earth was warm underfoot; the grass sprang high all up the hill and weedflowers nodded and lounged in it yellow and red and pale purple. Daff waded through them fast with the crying baby, and Oll went to meet him, almost laughing, he looked so frightened of the tiny mewling thing.

A Feather in the Breast of God

In memoriam: HG, Roy, Smoke, and Whitey

I arrived in moonlight; it wasn't hard to find the way. The cage was just as I'd left it, down to the droppings on the newspaper floor, black-and-white glisters with long moon shadows. There was no water, and something was wrong with the food from being so old.

I waited in the middle of the perch, mostly tranced, saving my energy, with my "head" under my "wing" so that I looked like a normal bird sleeping. It was a day or so. I could hear them in there, voices and thumps, pad-padding back and forth. I heard Scarlet's voice, definitely, once or twice. But they didn't come out, and now that I was down here I didn't have the overview I'd had. I remembered I used to be bored when I was entirely bird; I used to greet them all, relieved, when they came out. But in this state there's no such thing as boredom; the passing of time is interesting enough in itself.

Flights of lorikeets came through on the way to the pine seeds and the black bean tree. I would have liked to join them, just to stretch my wings again. But such visits as mine are very circumscribed; every movement must be in relation to a prior Connection—or at least directed to a tangible good. And I was never Connected to those birds.

Cats, now . . . well, there were plenty of cats. One came and watched me for long spells, a big orange thing. That would have used to make me go all still and nervous. My "body" remembered that stillness, my "heart" hammered. But the main part of me wasn't afraid of such things anymore.

In the end I said to it, "I have already been eaten by one of you."

It puffed up all fat and stiff-legged.

"Why don't you go and find a real bird?" I told it.

The cat shot away up the garden, looked back at me, fled up the fence, checked me again. I oughtn't to have spoken, I suppose. But really, it would have starved itself, sitting and waiting for me. I was sure it would feel tangibly good at its first bite of tin-food.

I started to need water. Without it, the light seemed to turn against me; the garden bushes were full of disturbances; those junior magpies ambling on the grass, I imagined their eyes to be full of intentions they could not have. For some hours it was all I could do not to fly out as I had before—only instead of giving myself up to the teeth of the world, instead of being caught on a claw and crushed in a mouth, I would forsake this scrap of hungry earthliness I had borrowed and return to my place on the god's breast, free again of all dangers and lesser desires.

The boy, Taylor, that I used to sit on the shoulder of, he was the first out, and he saw me straightaway.

"Hey." He stopped with his laundry bundle, which was like several big, multicolored cats knotted together. He backed away to the open door. "Hey, Mum," he called through it. "Smoko's back."

I heard her voice, disbelieving.

"Come and look," cried Taylor. "Come and shut his door on him. I can't reach."

He waited there until she came.

"Oh my goodness, so he is," she said.

"Like I'd make *that* up." He went to the basket behind her as she closed the cage door. The scent on her fingers, and the smell of his sockery and pantery breaking open, nearly knocked me off the perch.

A human eye is bigger than the head of a bird like me, if you take into account all the parts behind their eyelids. When it looks at you, it's hard to think straight, for fear of where all that attention might lead.

Mum opened the door again and reached her sweet, sweet, powerful fingers in. I flung against the far bars, I was so startled and faint.

"Poor old Smoko," she said. "Let me get rid of this moldy old thing for you. Here, Tay, scrub this out and fill it with some clean water."

"Where've you been, Smoko?" said Taylor in a special pray-ing voice. "Have you had an egg-venture?"

"What I want to know is what brought him *back*." Mum held the noisome seed stick away to one side. "How he *survived*, for one, and how he found his way back here." And then she prayed to me: "There's more in that little brain than meets the eye, bird, isn't there? You're not as dim as you sum, are you?"

After that things fell into place better. The water came.

"Look, he's thirsty!"

"He's going for it! Just putting his head down and guzzling!"

They also brought some very good greens, a great bunch of them. I had much to concentrate on, working the beak and tongue, remembering the innards and the old satisfactions of how they worked.

Mum and Taylor took me into the house, just as they used to, because evening was falling. They put fresh paper below me and sat around marveling.

"Maybe it's *not* Smoko," said Taylor. "Maybe it's another budgie that looks like him."

"Well, that would almost be more likely. When was it we lost him?"

They tried to work that out. Finally they arrived at the four weeks by remembering that they'd been on the way to the Easter Show; the bigger boy, Ethan, had been hurrying and for-gotten to close the cage; they'd bought a mirror at the Show that Smoko had never got to use. I sat up at that, but from what they said, they'd given the mirror away.

All this was very interesting, but it was not what I was here for. Where had the girl gone? I guessed she was at that man's place, but I couldn't see from here. I had lost perspective. My birdly anxieties said, *She could be anywhere, hopped on a plane and anywhere.* I didn't have all the time in the world.

And now the cage door was closed and I was limited in movement, unless I left this body behind—and it's a serious job to make a body that will function discreetly in the Hereunder. Once it's made, it's best to stay with it, not pop in and out as if it were a birdbath.

"Good night, Smoko," they prayed, and covered me with a cloth smelling of their laundry perfume. Soon the light stopped showing through the cloth, and silence fell, each one deeper than the previous—first the family, then their laundry machine, then the neighbors, then the plane traffic, then the road, then the rail. There was tippy-tapping of a few mice; a rat ran by, but did not come inside; those big black insects scrittled over floor and wall and table. One came and investigated, but I hissed at it and it went away. I never liked those things—bad enough sitting over your mess all night without those things scratching and nibbling it as well.

I settled eventually, more or less, although secretive cat's paws went over the roof all night and made me stir. Ethan came into the house, and toileted and ran water and gulped it down. I kept quiet and he didn't even look under the cloth.

Scarlet would have visited this room, had she been home at all; she might be sliding uncontrolled toward a Defining Moment, but her appetite wasn't affected—or hadn't been, up to the time I took birdly form and Descended.

I tried to tuck myself away in a trance again, but my brain would keep worrying. Scarlet could have gone anywhere, done anything; she was an angry girl—and for no reason! She had a lovely mum, and Mum and Taylor and Ethan together formed a wonderful bosom for her, to all intents and purposes uncondi-tional in their love. Why she should want to lever herself out of that bosom and stalk away into the cold and the chemicals, who knew? That man, he was no sort of reason at all. A ball of black-ness wrapped in handsome paper, he was—even Scarlet could put her finger through him if she had a mind to. Which of course she didn't—she was very much set the other way, to not see things, to not protect herself. She was all biology: *get away and mate*, her body was telling her. Last thing she wanted was to think sensibly.

How was I going to do this thing? The water in my drinking dripper was too small to put a simulacrum through. If they hung me by a window, maybe I could use the glass. If I was outside and it rained, or a hose leaked a puddle. If they kept me in the kitchen and left me alone, if there was a drink on the bench, or if they wiped the sink shiny enough, maybe I could see through and find her and go to work.

All the long next day, hanging by the laundry, I waited and pondered. Funny how when it's not wanted, some reflective sur-face is always winking, throwing out irrelevant scenes and voices, making it hard to eat. Yet when there is a task to accom-plish, all is matte and movement. The only hope I had that whole long day was when Mum hung out some Scarlet clothes, like thick black spiderwebs clamped to the lines. *There, the girl will come back to collect those. But then, sometimes Mum washes things, and packs them in a bag, and takes them up to the box by the railway station.* And I was all doubtful and anxious again.

Mum took me indoors late that afternoon, and there was a lot of praying and swinging and uncertainty just about that. Then Scarlet came in, all of a sudden and smelly with smoke and train smells and the pa-choury she's started burning at the man's place. She pushed past Mum at the door, to get to her spiderwebs on the line.

"Well, and good *morning* to you, too," said Mum.

"Hi, Mu-u-um," said Scarlet in her boredest voice, un-pegging.

Mum gathered herself to start talking, but then the house filled with arriving Taylor and arriving Ethan, so she didn't.

Taylor thundered straight through from the far entry, shouting. He flung himself across the table at me and swung something bright from his hand. "Do you like it, Smoke? Do you like the look of yourself? Are you beautiful?" he prayed.

"Oh," said Mum. "Did you get it back from Marina?"

"This isn't *ours*." It was Taylor's best withering voice. "Ours was *orange*, remember, with *beads*. Marina's dad got this one. I was telling Marina this morning about Smoko coming back, and I didn't say she had to give it back or anything, but her dad heard. And *he* didn't say anything, but when he came to pick her up he had this, because—"

"Are you *sure* you didn't say anything? Anything that would make them feel guilty?"

"No-o! You ask him! He said Wellington got so much joy out of the mirror we gave him—"

"Is that what he said— 'got so much joy'?" Mum was smiling now—I only just managed to notice it, through the noise and the swinging light and the general discombobulation, and trying to keep a hold on the whereabouts of Scarlet.

"Yes! He said he couldn't bear to think of any budgie going without a mirror. He said sorry there aren't any beads; he said the lady in the shop said—"

Whack! went the door on the wall and in came Scarlet, trailing her webs through the kitchen. She stopped Ethan at the bathroom door, sweeping past so imperiously.

"Oops," he said, and that was all. I like Ethan—he's a kind boy, really, for all he pretends to be an angry boofhead.

Into the silence Mum said, "Well, that was very nice of him. What's his name again, Marina's dad?"

"*I* don't know."

Juan, I thought, to stop myself feeling sick. *Juan Antonio Jimenez*. A bird brain can't hold much and keep it straight.

Mum closed the whacked door. "Put it in the cage," she said, "so he can start to *get some joy* out of it."

I backed away. Taylor's hand, smelling of play dirt and lollies, came in and hung the mirror at the far end of the perch. It was the perfect size, if a bit—

"It's a bit smudgy," said Ethan. "He won't be able to see himself in that."

Taylor took the mirror out again, breathed on it, and polished it ("Not on your *school* shirt, Taylor—use a tissue!" "It's *fine*, Mum!"), then hung it back. *Now* it was perfect.

When the hand withdrew I sidled up the perch.

"Look, he loves it already!"

"Who's that new bird, Smoke? Who is it?"

" 'Now, did I part my feathers right this morning?' "

I pecked at the simulacrum a couple of times to make sure it was working properly. Behind it Scarlet was clearly visible in her room, packing all manner of black clothing into the bag that used to be her school bag.

" 'What a beautiful bird!' "

" 'Stunning. Gorgeous.' "

" 'I think I'm in lurv!' "

I wouldn't be able to do anything with the family around. I disguised my irritation with some grooming. Frightening a cat is one thing; showing your true nature to your Connected Souls—well, you can do it in an emergency, but frivolous exposures can have consequences you might not want to deal with.

" 'Yes, I could do with a bit of a tidy-up.' "

"That's right, Smoke. Make yourself nice for your girl-friend."

"Bet you didn't meet anyone as cute as that on your travels."

It's best just to wait when they carry on like this. It doesn't usually last long.

But even when they stopped they were distracting, making their dinner, eating around the table, breaking into prayer if I made a move. I put my head under my wing as a hint, but they wouldn't put the cloth over me. They didn't talk about anything useful, either—Scarlet barely entered the conversation, let alone importantly. She and Mum must have had words while I was transmigrating; things must have come to a head. That was good timing on my part. I didn't like to watch them fighting from above; I saw inside them too clearly, to all their pains and rages. But I'd be able to do some good while the feelings were all stirred up and tender.

I glimpsed Scarlet through the mirror, during dinner, running for the train, then sitting grooming her dark purple claws, painting her dark purple lips darker. Where she got off it was raining, hard to read the wet ground and all those extra lights. Then—after a bit of praying, Mum *finally* put my cloth on—she was at the man's house.

He was on the phone—for a long time, talking trash, two low-worth people talking together, further lowering both their selves. She waited, at first irritably, but then she went farther into the house, from room to room, looking at everything but not touching. He didn't like that—when it was clear she hadn't just gone to the bathroom he came out to the hall and frowned about, and when next he saw her he beckoned. She skipped away into the bathroom then, and while his voice and his pretend laughter boomed in the hall she went piece by piece through the marvels of his bath cabinet, touching and lifting only as much as she needed to, to see what was what.

There was a rustle of my cloth, then an eye, then the cloth again. "Yep," Ethan said. "Still admiring himself."

"Telling himself a bedtime story," said Taylor. "'Once upon a time there were three poor budgies, living in a forest.'"

By the time they'd got out of my tail feathers Scarlet was back with the man, the phone was unplugged from the wall, and the glassware was all laid out in its ceremonial array, the only clean thing in the house, kept that way so it wouldn't contaminate the chemical.

Scarlet sat watching, luminous, her eyes beautiful with fear.

He loved that, the man. It gave him flourish. To be the knower, in front of such innocence and curiosity. He'd already done it with the sex; now he wanted to do it with the substances. He wanted to claim more and more, until she was hurt, and wept, until she was wrecked and ruined. She thought it was love, but he wouldn't know love from a hole in the ground. *He* thought this was love, too, this wreckage. When it was complete, he would say she had spoiled the love, that he had brought it to her pure and she had fussed and spoiled it with her neediness.

"Roll up your sleeve," he said, and handed her the tightener. "Put this on."

I pecked at the simulacrum and we groomed ourselves, just quickly, just to make sure we were ready in every covert and pinion. Beyond my fellow there the work went on, with the flame and the precious dust and the injecting machine. Nothing spilled or was wasted. The man kept his temper; he didn't loose a single dungword. Scarlet stayed still and wide-eyed.

I sent the simulacrum down. It put chin to chest and dropped and spread and fluttered, onto Scarlet's shoulder. It had a finer body than I; being invisible, it could afford to be ideal— there was no risk that it would dazzle and unhinge anyone.

Scarlet turned its way and searched the shadows behind her. The simulacrum breathed, and fanned its breath into her face.

"Tighter!" snapped the man.

Scarlet fumbled with the tightener. Bright droplets of the

substance-juice sprang from the needle, curved on the air—apparently it was all right to waste just this little, to make this little libation.

Taylor trained Smoko first to sit on his finger. He carried him around, finger to shoulder to finger.

He sat at the computer and the bird sat with him.

He brought Smoko into Scarlet's room, where she was studying. She looked up scowling, but the scowl cleared when she saw the bird. "Will he come to me?" she said.

"He'll come to anything that bumps him in the chest," said Taylor.

Scarlet touched the breast feathers with her knuckle and up Smoko stepped.

"Oh," she said. "His feet are *warm!*"

"Well, look at them; they're so pink, they'd have to be."

She laughed carefully, through her nose. "I don't know. I expected them to be cold and scratchy. Like a reptile's. To *hurt!* But yes, you're toasty, aren't you?"

Smoko sat in a general gentle tremble of nerves, weighing very little.

The simulacrum hardly looked like a budgerigar at all. Its head was hidden by the wings that cut and cupped the air like a courting riflebird's. Its breath found Scarlet's ear and nose. She watched the man's face and her lips parted, and the breath went in there, too. The simulacrum's tail was spread around her shoulder for balance.

The man took her arm smoothly, her white, woman's arm. In the elbow the vein rose purple, plump with clean blood. The strain of keeping up the simulacrum made my thinking go all timeless and godlike: here was that little crooked limb forming in the darkness of the mum, cell by cell; here it wavered, white, needing to grasp and bring every object to the mouth; here, longer, it worked busily at its learning; scrawny and tanned, here it hauled ropes at the boat they made at the beach that summer, the summer she thought was the time of her life, that she wouldn't get better than, now that she was self-conscious. Through the wingbeats, as through a slatted blind being opened and closed, on the far side of this moment all the possibilities fanned out in the usual array, none of them "better" or "worse," if we're talking Intrinsics, than any other, whether the arm be withered inside an old-lady cardigan in a rest home, or fuller and starting to sag, clasped around her own child's teenage shoulders, or still shapely with youth, black-tracked and lamplit and lifeless, fallen from curb to gutter. They shifted about, all these might-be's, in front of one another to form the general mud of that phenomenon mortals call the future, that they choose and don't choose, that they make or stumble into, or have thrust on them.

I thought all this in the moment it took the man to bring down the instrument. In the lamplight, from behind the mirror, it was a thing of beauty, as if he were applying a piece of jewelry to her skin, or placing one of the more decorative insects there—a scarab, a Christmas beetle, a mantid with a fresh new skin. She could go either way, even with the breath on her, even with the simulacrum on her shoulder making its own kind of beauty, matching with its cool holy love the exciting new weirdness of the man's handsome pretense.

He pushed the needle in, through the so-soft skin. The simulacrum snapped back to itself and cocked its head to watch.

The man paused a moment. I'll give him that—it might be the one thing that saves him in the end from the Ceaseless Pain, from the Eternal Deterioration of the Damned. With the needle in the flow, and the chemical dissolved and ready, he lifted his eyes to hers.

The simulacrum re-set its head, lifted one wing, and blew along it a single rolling ball of breath that burst against Scarlet's white neck and spilled all about, up into her carefully tangled hair, down across the wrinkled dark purple cloth of her breast, down past the label of her clothing at the back, and trickling down the soft warm indentations of her spine.

"No," she said.

Nothing moved but their eyes.

"You're sure?" said the man.

"Yes. I mean, yes, I'm sure."

"I know what I'm doing. I won't give you too much. And it's pure; I've had it myself. It's good stuff."

"No, take it out. I don't want to."

He took it out—again, he could have forced her, he could have squeezed some in. I don't know for certain she'd have pulled away. Maybe there is hope for him after all?

He shrugged, and gestured for the tightener. She watched him, pulling down her raggy sleeve, not noticing the escaped bead of blood smearing on her skin. The simulacrum flew from her shoulder, straight for the mirror.

"You'll have all of it?" she said. "You were only going to have half. Will you be all right?"

The man smiled—any girl might be taken in by that weathered, carefree face. "I was only going to go for a little ride. Out of politeness—your first time and everything."

He did it to himself, then—to his own vein in his own arm, which was far beyond my powers of protection. He sat back in the big scratchy armchair, and sank away from her. He came back for a moment, to tell her how good it was, then fell away again.

She watched the whites of his eyes. She picked up the instrument and turned its emptiness over in her hands. The simulacrum perched low opposite me, peering into the cage, wanting home now that its work was done.

The man's mouth had fallen open. Water pooled inside the lower lip, ready to drool out. "It's not very interesting from the *outside*, that's for sure," Scarlet murmured. She stood, picked up her bag.

I stayed with her as far as the street, then summoned the simulacrum back through. The moment we were incorporated, I slept.

In my dream I rose through to the Hereabove, a single flake or feather traveling upward on the indrawn breath of the god-who-admits-of-love. There curved its breast above me, densely feathered with souls. The freshly dead ones who had been kept and cared for on earth, they were the brightest; others whose Connections with the Hereunder were dying one by one were being resorbed, fading into the body of the god. All was warmth and light; earthly sensations fell away, the twitching fear, the gnawing hunger and thirst, the thinned-out feeling that tiredness gives you. My borrowed body's false feathers with all their mites and dust dropped behind me, my bones heavy with earthly air, as I flew without beat of wing or heart toward the place reserved for me on the god's skin.

I woke in a panic. A dark-clawed hand pursued me. Bars beat on my wings, on the back of my head.

They were the cage, and the claw was the hand of Scarlet, looming there in all her multifarious layers and odors.

"Come on," she prayed. "You used to hop on anyone's hand."

"Leave him alone," said Taylor in his pajamas at the door, rubbing one eye. "You have to tame them up again—they don't remember. You have to do it every day, and it's been four weeks since he practiced."

"Well, whoever had him should've kept him up to speed." But she pulled her hand away, and closed the door, and dropped the cloth.

"Maybe nobody had him. Maybe he was living wild and free."

"Bull, he was. He'd've been cat food in two seconds if he hadn't found another home."

They squabbled on, and I smoothed myself down. I lost a few feathers in the preening; now that the Defining Moment had passed, the form would not last long. I would be gone by morning from this itchy, seedy world full of frights, flown to the bosom of the god.

I fluffed up what was left of me and settled beside the dark mirror.

Hero Vale

Diammid Anderson gazed over into the Vale. It was dark down there among the trees, and not just from shadow. He was glad of the rock's coolness and solidity against his chest.

"I don't like that black mist," he said. "It makes me feel as if bits of my eyes are blind."

"Oh, you caint see straight in this place," said Razor. "And when you *do* see summink, afterwards you caint quite remember. You caint quite believe, you know? It will not stay proper in your head."

Razor's skin was like yellowed wax. He was dressed all in raggy black, his head thrust forward motionless, his miserable eyes taking in the overcast sky, the complex darkness of the Vale.

"It's not guaranteed we'll see anything at all, is it?" said Diammid.

"Nuffink's sure, no. Git out the glass, though—you never know, it might help."

Diammid had forgotten about the spyglass. He rummaged in the rucksack and brought it out. It was comforting to look at, and to hold—the old tooled red leather, the chased metal.

"Crothel will notice it's gone. Maybe even before he notices *me* gone." Diammid laughed nervously.

"Long as we get us a half hour here. Any longer and we'll be for the nuthouse."

"Have you ever stayed longer?"

"Last time I stayed an hour, but half of that I was behind this rock, not looking, while Ark and Chauncey went peculiar. I had to whack them in the end, to get them away."

"I heard that Ark hardly had any nose left."

"I dint do that. The other boy done that. Fighting like scranny cats, they were."

"Is it true, then—they only hurt each other? Nothing else got to them, from down there?"

"Ennink from *down there*," said Razor with a bitter smile, "the boy wouldn't be alive, I don't reckon."

It's not possible, Tregowan had said. *I saw Ark. No one the size and make of Thomas Chauncey could do such damage. His ear was torn near right* off.

Diammid hadn't seen either boy right afterward. By the time he'd got back from hockey practice Ark was gone to the hospital, all the way to London, and his parents shipped him home from there; Chauncey had been fetched from the school San and kept home six weeks. He had come back cold and quiet and no longer popular, lasted to the end of summer term, and then gone away for good.

Diammid glanced at Razor again. The older boy's eyes were like pale gray buttons; his mouth was always pursed as if he were remembering some new thing to worry about. He was one of those people who would go through to old age with barely a change; he would wrinkle up a little and his dull brown hair would go gray, but that would be all. And then he would die. Diammid rarely thought about deaths like Razor's; he suppressed a shiver, and turned back to the Vale. "There *are* colors," he said. "Just not strong ones. Just very dim greens and browns, and you have to look for them."

"They might stren'then, if summink comes," said Razor. "They tend to."

"You never properly said what you've seen," said Diammid.

"Shh," said Razor. He had not shifted his gaze from the Vale.

A peculiar feeling flowed off Diammid's last words to Razor, *You never properly said . . .* It hissed off Razor's *shh* and moved across Diammid's mind like the black mist down there, which had just covered a patch of tree trunks, tangling with the beardy stuff in the lower branches. Razor is lying, he knew all of a sudden. He's faking. He's making it up. He's never seen anything here. He just—

Then the mist passed, showing the tree trunks again, the beards, the white haze of the beardberries. And Razor's eyes were steady; they didn't dart guiltily or anything suspicious. And Razor hadn't taken the money Diammid had offered him on Wednesday, had just looked at him by the roadside there where accosted and said, *Course I'll take you, if you're sure.* And pushed Diammid's hand away, with the money in it. *No,* he'd said. *It's not a thing I do for money.*

Razor turned and saw the stare on Diammid. "Have a bite," he said. "It's best not to be hungry. But be quiet about it. And keep looking. More eyes the better."

Diammid pulled out the cloth full of chicken fritters, fresh tuck swapped from a day boy. He handed one to Razor and bit into another.

Oh, there was nothing like eating outside; there was nothing like striding away from Grammar and going somewhere one shouldn't go, and then eating; there was nothing like salty yellow-and-brown fritter full of shredded white meat and glossy green peas; Diammid only just restrained himself from grunting with pleasure as he ate. My heaven, it was good.

You wouldn't, Teasdale had sneered across the supper table.

Would too, said Diammid—it was easily said.

You wouldn't have the bottle. You're just another spineless tweaker from Roscoe's dorm, all farts and giggles. His cronies laughed like machine guns, showing half-chewed food.

Yet here he was, scoffing fritter above Hero Vale. And when Teasdale heard he'd gone, he wouldn't believe it at first, but then he'd have to. Diammid hoped someone was watching, and could tell him later about the look on Teasdale's face.

Who will vouch for this boy, Rickets? For this worm? For this weed?

Bully Raglan rowed and boxed and played rugby. He and all his lads were big, stuffed tight with muscles, excepting Arthur

Septimus, who was tiny and weaselly and did all Bully's listening and spying. Bully strutted about in the quad, ridiculous in his short pants and braces. Diammid wondered at how such a big baby-looking boy could make the whole quadful of boys stiffen and stink with fear.

Teasdale and his boys were up on the hall balcony, jostling and egging Bully on.

Rickets was white and his eyes were lowered; there was a spot of pee on the front of his shorts from when Bully Raglan had grabbed him so suddenly out of the huddle of new Preps.

What happens if no one vouches for him? whispered a Prep behind Diammid.

He will destroy him, is what Hopper says.

What, beat him up?

Well, that too.

No one? cried Bully. *Rickets is alone in the world? Rickets is entirely without protection?* He smirked. *And such a fine figure of a man, too. Shall we see just how fine?* he called up to Teasdale's lads.

Show us his haunches! they cried out. *Show us his scrawny chest!*

They won't, will they? Diammid thought unhappily. They won't take off his clothes?

Rickets slowly raised his face, the face of a boy who was always smallest and palest and most picked upon. Diammid saw not only that they would strip Rickets and worse, but that Rickets knew they would, knew and was already resigned, so resigned he was almost saintly with it, sagging in his captor's arms, reading his future in Bully's bully eyes.

Razor touched Diammid's elbow. He was staring, caught in mid-chew, toward the far rim of the Vale.

Diammid swallowed; a big lump of fritter went down unappreciated. Here it was, then, the sight he'd come to see, the tale he'd come to fetch and take back to Grammar and widen the fellows' eyes, and quieten Teasdale a minute.

Copper and emerald brightened in a high part of the forest thick with the mist, almost boiling with it. Then the mist passed, and the copper gleamed, and the emerald turned and flashed, and there was some shape to the thing.

"Is that the head?" Diammid muttered. "That *whole thing's* the head? But how far away . . ."

"Arr, gawd," said Razor through fritter. "Always when I bring you Grammar lads. I come by myself and all I see is elefumps or horned horses that stray out and wander and stray back. But that's a full hero, that one. The real thing. Oh, my."

"That's good, isn't it?"

"Might be good, if we keep very, very still. Might just look about a bit and pass on. That's what Mr. Ark's and Mr. Chauncey's did. Set them against each other summink terrible, but it didn't do aught itself."

In shape and solidity the head was like a cauldron, or maybe a boat, a high-sided coracle. It looked as if it were made of iron, iron covered with a coppery skin. Its thin, shiny black hair was tied behind; one ear was clear for a moment, intricate, with coppery gleams inside. Diammid didn't want to look at the face. He turned his own face away, but his eyes would keep on looking. The hero's nose and mouth were small and delicate, almost pretty. But the eyes above the great broad cheeks, sitting on the cheekbones like plates propped on a mantel, were wide and indistinct. The gray irises slid and jittered, shrank and swelled on the vast, wet whites.

"Euh," said Diammid.

Razor's hand touched his arm again behind the rock. "Nought sudden," he murmured, and resumed chewing very slowly.

The hero moved, from the upper right of their view down through the trees toward the middle of the Vale.

"Is it *just* a head, floating?" said Diammid.

Razor swallowed. His voice came much clearer, but much quieter. "There's a body. Watch. Where there's less mist."

The head coasted down the hillside, closing its eyes and pushing its face through branches, or looking from side to side in a slow, wavering, oversized way. *Something* hung from its underside, some dark spindliness, some bright metal.

Slowly, behind the rock, and with his eyes on the floating head, Diammid pulled the glass open to its full length.

"Ooh," said Razor. Diammid could hardly hear him. "I'm not so sure about that now. With this one."

"Just to see that body, the nature of it." Slowly Diammid raised the glass to his eye.

"Mmph." Razor shifted uneasily.

"Phaugh, you should see this, Razor!" Diammid whispered. "It's just like us, only all streakly and straggly. *Weird.* Like dangling iron. But—what's that on its back?" He took his eye from the glass and checked, then put it back.

"I wouldn't be looking through that," whispered Razor. "I don't know—"

"Why, it's a shield! Great long thing. And his swords! See how they flash, their curved blades? Ooh, you should see the hilts of them. And he's got knives at his waist, and an ax, and— What are those beady things hanging from his belt?"

"Shh! Put it down, master," Razor hissed. "He's coming clearer. I'm sure you can see him just as well with your own eye now."

Diammid took down the glass and scowled into the Vale. The hero had paused in a clearing, about to plunge into a part of the Vale where the trees grew taller than himself. His heavy head turned and nodded, choosing the way. The head moved first and the slender body swung and drifted after it, brandishing its swords.

Diammid put the glass to his eye again. "I just want to see—"

"Master, I wouldn't."

The hero's head swiveled dozily toward them.

"Oh, look at the earring! It's—"

Diammid's eager voice switched off, as suddenly as if by electricity. Diammid was gone from beside Razor. The red leather spyglass hung where he had held it. Comb marks streaked the air where he had stood. Swirls at the other end showed the force with which he had been sucked through.

The glass dropped, *clink-tap-clink,* and rolled, and lay. Smoke wisped out at the top; a trickle of molten orange glass ran out the bottom and pooled on the rock.

Psst! Anderson! said the coatrack.

What? Diammid stared. *Who's that?*

A coat kicked out with a thin bruised leg, and now he saw the eye in the shadows. *Rickets?*

The boy hung there like a hunchback by the collar of his blazer. *Can you get me down, Anderson?*

Yes, but they'll— But I'll— Is it Bully has done this, or Teasdale?

Just for a piss, Anderson, and then you can hang me up again. Please. *I'm* busting. *It won't take a minute.*

Oh, all right. And he lifted the boy down and waited there, nervously. It took more than a minute, but eventually Rickets came hurrying into sight. *Quickly! I can hear them coming back from Gym!*

And it was accomplished.

Thanks, Anderson. Rickets pulled the coats around himself. *I owe you. Go away, now—you'd best not be found here.*

Diammid went, trying to shake off the scrape of Rickets's boot against his shin, the imprint of his bony hip as he lifted him down, the pale face with the watery greenish eyes, the smell of drains about the boy.

Bells rang above Diammid. His eyes would not open.

It seemed to him that he had only just been born. A great amber eye had brought him into being. He had started as a hot line on the air, then suddenly, violently been plumped into shape and thrown down on this grass. And now he was a dense honeycomb of pain, his every cell outlined with fire.

The hero's towering shadow darkened Diammid's eyelids. The black mist came and went. When it was there, it furred everything—sound and taste and skin—like iron filings on a magnet. It made the bells at the hero's waist clank and clack; when it cleared they rang sweet and properly metal.

*　*　*

Diammid's cheerful voice chimed across the supper table.

Where they come from, they come from other worlds. Where they go, they go back to other worlds; I don't know whether back to those they came from, or on to fresh ones, or what.

What do you mean, what other worlds? Teasdale scoffed. *You talk so much rot, Anderson: why don't you run orf and write one of your po-wems or something?*

I'm telling you, I talked to Razor; he told me.

He filled your head with gumf, is what. Razor is a filthy peasant what has et one toadstool too many. You there, pass the bread-and-dripping.

But why don't they come here?

What do you mean, Rickets?

When they're in our world. Why don't they do anything here? Come over to Grammar and—I don't know—flatten Raglan for us? Rickets finished under his breath. *Flatten that one.* He nodded faintly toward Teasdale, who was biting bread and calling up the table to someone.

Oh, they never come out of the Vale. Least, that's what Razor says. The sides are too steep, maybe. I don't know; I've never been there.

And you never will. There was Teasdale again. *You piece of slop.*

Diammid's eyelids unstuck from each other. The hero's booted iron legs led up to the bells and blades at his waist, to his swords in their battered black sheaths, to the head that blotted out so much of the sky.

87

"S-sir." Diammid's whole painful body trembled.

Ah. The hero's head tilted, the boots stepped away, the giant eyes came down. First the painful amber eye regarded him through the mist, then the other slewed gray across the eyeball, seeming to see nothing.

The hero opened his neat mouth. Diammid sensed a much larger, rawer mouth opening somewhere nearby.

Gorwr hay sheen hee pashin drouthsh, the hero said. Then both his eyes turned amber as the mist thickened, and he tried again: *You hay seen hee passin throok.*

The mist furred Diammid's eyes and brain. The hero was saying several things: *You have seen me passing through this place,* as well as *You have seen things you were not intended to see.* But most urgently the hero wanted to know, *Have you seen him? Which way did he pass?*

"Who, sir?" cried Diammid, but the mist had frayed and faded, and only the gray, uncomprehending eye swerved and slid above him. Diammid felt ill watching it—at any moment he would be sick all over the hero's boots.

But then the eye flickered and steadied amber again. Crothel had a piece of Baltic amber in the glass case in the Science Room; there was a lacewing trapped in it, with some scraps of ancient leaf litter. That specimen was a poor approximation of the amber world into which these eyes were windows. A dragonfly hung there, its thorax the length of Diammid's arm; whole thorny lizards hovered, wrinkled-leather birds with tooth-edged beaks, entire mammoths—bubbles clung to their flanks and crevices, golden with the hero's interior fire.

"Who, sir?" Diammid said again, to stop himself dying of the sight.

This time the hero understood. *Mine enemee.* His voice rumbled in the ground. Skulls hung on cords at his waist, skulls of wolves and of Diammid-sized people and of horned, toothed beasts Diammid did not recognize. They clacked and clinked together on many notes. *My foe!* The mist thinned, the words turned to roar, the eye dimmed and slithered, and the ground shook hard, banging against the back of Diammid's head. The hero blurred against the clouds, and the skulls became dull metal bells, and swung and sang.

Then the amber eye burned above him. *You cain tell me*, said the hero, *into whuchaputchatha . . .* The eye dimmed, then shone very bright and hot. *Into which aperture did he flee?*

"I have seen no one but yourself today, sir." Diammid trembled, pinned to the ground by the heat.

And other days? Many years might pass in this place, that do not signify for the duration of the chase. The eye came closer and hotter. Diammid squirmed.

"But I have never been here before, sir!"

I could crush your head like an asp's under my boot-heel, rumbled the hero, pushing his face lower. *I could cut you apart and hang your still-living pieces in the trees. Do not toy with me.*

"Oh, but I'm not, sir! I wouldn't!"

The hero brought the full heat of his amber eyes to bear on Diammid. The boy's skin crisped and curled and flamed up like thin dry leaves. He arched on the ground. Screams forced themselves out of him, unconnected to his will.

Then the black mist closed in with a sifting sound. Diammid's skin rose into iron fur. The mist blotted out the sky; from here to high in the Vale behind him the air turned hollow, so that his cries echoed lostly. And *something* emerged into this hollowness, heavy, scrambling, tearing the vegetation, breathing hard and steadily.

The hero's head swung up to face that other, and his amber eyes glared and glowed. *Show yourself, coward!* He drew both swords; they *tzanged* and spat on the iron-rich air. The skulls at his waist clacked out a horrid laughter. The trees had turned to leafless bone on all sides.

He strode up the hill. His iron boot toe kicked Diammid in the side; his following foot caught Diammid's head a blow that exploded the world into fireworks. The boy lay gasping, the enemy crooned farther away and higher, the giant's swords whipped the weighty air, and the trees rattled and rubbed their bones with his passing.

It was nearly teatime and Rickets was dozing when Anderson pulled apart the coats and lifted him down from the coat-hook.

Rickets shook out the arms of his shirt and blazer, blinking up at Anderson, not daring to speak. Anderson seemed taller, thinner. His face was one big rough-featured scab, incapable of expression without cracking.

"I thought you were— Shouldn't you be in the San?" said Rickets.

Stillness and patience clarified the air around Anderson, spreading out from him like a pure oil.

"Thank you," Rickets finally said, in a muted voice.

Anderson jerked his head. *Come on.*

Rickets bobbed along uncertainly beside Anderson, then settled to walking. He longed to ask, *What happened to you in the Vale? What did you see? Will you ever tell, or was it too terrible?* But the blunt, crusted ruin of Anderson's face was too awesome; he could not quite bring himself to. And then they passed the last empty dorm and went up into the Prefects Wing.

These stairs, these halls, were richly scented with Taylors Imperial tea and woodsmoke and buttered toast. A carpet runner muffled their footfalls, and peaceable sounds came from behind each door—the clink of glassware, Victrola music winding up, assured voices in conversation.

They stopped at a door guarded by two big boys. Rowdier talk went on within. "I'm here to see Bully Raglan." Anderson's voice was a burned-out croak.

One of the guards gave a startled laugh, and Rickets stifled a gasp. No one called Raglan "Bully" in front of his lads.

But the guard knocked on the study door and stuck his head round. The talk paused inside. "Anderson's here to see you."

"Anderson?" Raglan's sharp voice shook Rickets like a gust of wind. Anderson's hand rested briefly on his shoulder.

"The boy who—the one who got burned."

"I thought he was unconscious!"

"Well, he's here, Raglan, and asking to see you."

Raglan gave some signal, and the guard opened the door wide.

Rickets stood on the threshold, his mouth sagging open. All was rich reds and browns in blazing candlelight. Every surface invited the hand, from curved polished wood to embossed wallpaper to gilded picture frame to plump velvet upholstery, to the rug on the floor, thick-napped, brightly patterned, quite unmarked by wear. The difference between this warm place and the scarred Prep Common Room with its mean coke fire made Rickets ache.

The prefects sat around a table that was crowded with a miniature city of silverware and porcelain. At its pinnacle rose a many-storied cake stand. Sweet buns gleamed and glittered on the lower levels; a merry-go-round—an entire *carnival*—of iced and cream cakes ornamented the top tray. Bully Raglan's bad-tempered face was all the uglier for peering at Anderson around such beauties.

The other prefects winced and goggled at the sight of the burned boy. Teasdale looked to Raglan to see how he ought to behave.

"What is it, Anderson?" Raglan was rattled but did not want to show it.

"I've come to vouch for Rickets."

Raglan's gaze touched Rickets for the merest fragment of a second. "Jolly good. But I'm having my tea, boy. Can't this wait?" His voice was smooth as cream after Anderson's croaking.

"I've come to vouch for any other Prep boy who needs protection from you, Bully Raglan."

A high giggle broke from Teasdale. The other prefects froze.

Raglan slowly, smoothly adjusted his head the way Rickets imagined a snake would, lining itself up ready to strike. "I beg your pardon?" he said almost soundlessly. "What did you call me, Anderson?"

"Bully, sir."

Only the faces changed. The prefects' slackened in disbelief; Bully's assembled like a fist. Even the cakes sat stiller on their stand.

Raglan was fast; he leaped around the table. But Anderson ran two steps and launched himself straight across it. Boy, vessels, and cloth disappeared on the far side. A cake flew out of the crashing to the underside of the marble mantel, stuck there, then fell, leaving a smear of cream.

The prefects exploded from their chairs, shouting.

"Collar him!" said Raglan. "Burns or not, I shall beat him senseless!"

Anderson had landed in the fire. Now he rose, the back of his dressing gown alight, the flames sheeting up behind his gruesome head. He dived again, between the prefects' odd-angled bodies and upflung hands, fetching up against the wall, the bulwark, the immovable might that was Bully Raglan.

And the wall buckled.

"Get him off me!" The bully tried to step back, but Anderson had a death grip around his knees. "Do something! Help me, you wasters." Batting at the boy's flaming back, the blond floss of his own hair catching fire, Raglan fell.

"It was *wonderful!*"

The circle of faces glowed back at Rickets in the faint light from around the dormitory window blind. Soft laughter warmed the air at his face.

"It *sounds* wonderful!"

"Oh, I wish I'd seen it. Raglan on fire and screaming!"

"Go on, Rickets. Don't stop there."

"Well, then they threw Raglan's smoking jacket on Anderson to smother the flames, so *that* was ruined. And they rolled him on the carpet, so there were these scorch marks. . . ." Rickets sighed with pleasure. "And then they called Matron because Raglan was making such a racket, and she made him look like a goose with that bandage, and the pre's had to carry Anderson back to the San on a blanket and, I tell you—"

"He was unconscious, wasn't he?"

"Yes! And he *stank* of burning, and he was *filthy*, covered in ash, and he was bleeding—his face, you know, where he had knocked the scabs—and all the—he must have fallen right *on* the cakes—he was all over jam and cream, and this big *splash* of tea down his nightshirt. He was soaked; he was a mess! And they carried him off in the blanket, and even with the mess and the cream and such, he was—I don't know—like a prince being carried on a litter, or maybe a soldier with his comrades bringing him off the battlefield, with the gunsmoke hanging in the air still. The noble dead, you know? The glorious dead." Rickets's whisper was breaking up with glee. "Lying there with his robe around him, and all these prefects his servants. It was—*perfect*. I can't tell you!"

"He didn't have permission to leave the San," said Lowthal.

"Really?" said Tregowan.

"He was supposed to be in bed, ordered by the doctor. O'Callaghan said he heard Matron say. She couldn't believe he walked that far, let alone got in a fight."

"Let alone *won*!"

Hands clapped softly or covered laughing mouths.

"So is he all brave because he went to the Vale?" chirped Crewitt Minor. "Is that what happens to you?"

"Well, it didn't happen to Chauncey and Ark, did it?" said Lowthal. "And that boy, the one who brought Anderson back—he's a weed, isn't he? He's a very quiet sort of person. I mean normally, not when he's blubbing and carrying on like he was then. Nothing brave or reckless about him, that I've heard of."

"He's mad in the head, is all. Anderson, I mean. He's sick. Delirious. Brain fever."

"Cave! Cox!" hissed Harvey at the door, and they scattered to their beds.

Mrs. Cox entered the suddenly silent dorm. She made one slow, suspicious patrol, sniffing and hmm-ing as if trying to decide which boy she would pounce on and sink her long teeth into. Lowthal gave a creditable snore, but—"Don't imagine I am fooled for one moment by you, James Lowthal," she said. And then she sat at the open door with her lamp, pointedly rustling the pages of her book.

Rickets lay full of his story, the darkness lit by the memory of that crowd of enthralled faces. Their owners fell asleep one by one around him. Things would be different now; things would be much improved, wouldn't they? Bully's reputation surely could not survive this? The whole of Grammar bubbled with laughter at him.

And if Raglan managed to live today down, if he came back stronger and crueler than ever, there would always be Diammid

Anderson with his awful face and the absolute certainty of his bearing. Anderson would always be there for the Preps; he had said so.

And even—Rickets breathed happiness into the night—even if he wasn't, even if Anderson died of his wounds, Rickets would have the memories to hearten him, of Anderson lifting him down from the coat-hook, of Anderson calling Bully "Bully" to his face, of Anderson rising to his bare toes, and running two light steps across the prefects' carpet, and taking flight over the laden table, and crashing to Rickets's, to *everyone's* rescue, in a magnificent explosion of cakes, and plate, and sparks, and shattering china.

Under Hell, Over Heaven

"You always have to go *through* stuff," said Barto. "Why couldn't somebody have made a road?"

Leah grunted. Yes, it was always a trudge here. But what was the hurry when it came to eternity? Might as well trudge as run. Might as well be hampered as not. Barto was new here; he didn't realize. He'd just arrived, and by car accident, so he was still in a kind of shock. He was trying to catch hold of the last threads of his curiosity as it disappeared.

Right now they were walking through reedy, rushy stuff, sometimes ankle-deep in black water. It was quite dim, too. They were deep in the Lower Reaches; Hell's crusted, warty underside hung low above them, close enough to feel the warmth. There were four of them: Leah, Barto, Tabatha, and King. They were all youngish, so far as that meant anything, and they spoke the same language, so they made a good team. Plus there was the Miscreant Soul they were escorting, on his string. At least he'd stopped moaning. Hard as it was to feel strongly for or against anything here, the Miscreant's carryings-on had managed to irritate Leah.

Well, it was entirely up to you, she'd said to him. *You can get away with a certain amount, but you can't expect to be forgiven everything.*

Why not? he'd retorted miserably. *What skin would it have been off anyone's nose?*

It's just not the way the system works, King had said. *The line has to be drawn somewhere.*

I don't see why.

You don't have to, said Leah. *It's not your business to see. Just count yourself lucky to get any glory at all. Some people never even catch a glimpse.* And she'd made sure to walk on the far side of the group after that, so his complaints were mostly lost on the warm, wet breeze.

He was naked, the Miscreant. He didn't get to keep the white garb and the little round golden crown. He was just a plump white man, rather the shape of a healthy baby, on a leash of greenish-yellow string and with his hands tied behind his back. He had died of a knifing outside his office building; the big wound that had opened him up from left shoulder to right hip was sealed up shiny pink.

The rest of them wore the gray-green uniform. It was neither shapeless nor quite fitted, neither long nor short, neither ugly nor attractive in worldly terms; it was not remarkable in any way unless—Leah had seen it on the Miscreant's face, on the face of the woman at the desk at Heaven Gate—you were used to that other uniform, the white one, and the beaming face above.

The woman had cleared her throat and some of the light had gone out of her face; when they were so close to the Gate, people didn't like to look away from it. *You have some business with us?*

Tabatha had handed over the satchel, and they'd all stood around as the woman went slowly through the leather pages. The occasional seal shone light up into her face, but she looked less and less happy the more she read.

This is never good. She'd slapped the satchel closed. *This is never a pleasant task. Do you have the appropriate device?*

Tabatha had held up the two lengths of string—Leah saw King's fingers rub together, and her own tingled at the memory of rolling the grass fibers into string on her thigh. The woman on the desk had sighed and stood and crossed the little bit of marble paving in front of the Gate.

"Someone up ahead," said King. "It looks like a staffer. With a crook?"

Leah looked up from the reeds and the water. Yes, there was the curl of a crozier against the gray sky ahead.

"He's coming right for us," said Barto. "Of course, I don't mind if it's not *specifically* for me."

The man was tall, as a Shepherd should be. "All hail!" he

cried as soon as he saw them. No one spoke as he toiled forward through the swishing reeds.

He patted the satchel on his white-robed hip. "I have papers here for an infant, Jesus Maria Valdez."

There was a slight sag among the four of them at the word *infant*. The Miscreant narrowed his eyes at the staffer. So he had been hopeful, too.

"There are a lot of infants back there," said Leah. "Get through this boggy stretch; look out for a copse of dark trees on your right. They're in there, on the ground and up among the branches, heaps of them."

He was on his way. "I'll try there," he called back over his shoulder. "Praise be."

"Whatever," said Barto softly. Oh, he minded a great deal.

Leah shook herself and walked on. Out here, you got to know too well all the different shades of disappointment.

"What was that all about?" said the Miscreant, watching the glittering crozier recede. "Someone *else's* paperwork got mixed up?"

"Probably a posthumous baptism," said King. "Or an intercession, you never know. They don't have friends, babies, but sometimes there's a very devout grandmother. Come on." He tugged the string gently.

The Miscreant resumed his trudging. "So that baby gets to Ascend?"

Leah didn't hear any answer—she was watching reeds and water again—but the Miscreant asked no more, so someone must have nodded.

Actually, Hell would be so much worse for the Miscreant,

now that he'd been inside Heaven Gate and experienced that eternity. It would be worse than it would have been for Leah herself, who had only seen the Light, only felt it, from here in the Outer, and only for a few seconds at a time. And it was hard enough for her, this ache that never left her bones, this endless dull knowledge that things weren't as they should be.

They came to the edge of the marsh, up onto a rise covered with brown grass. There were quite a few people there. Two groups prayed to a Wrong God, the women wearing headcloths woven laboriously from grass fibers—where did they get the energy for the praying, for the weaving? Babies floated here and there in their greenish swaddling, some sleeping, some awake and waving their arms, kicking their legs; another one screamed inconsolably in the distance. Other people wandered alone, meeting no one's eye, or lay on the grass looking up at the carbuncular ceiling, which was just like the surface of Heaven, except that it rumbled occasionally, and leaked dirty yellow puffs of sulfur.

Leah's party passed on into the grasslands. The going was drier, but pricklier underfoot, and the grasses had sharp edges that made long, light cuts on their bare legs.

"You never know, do you," said Barto quietly at her shoulder. "You see a bloke with a cut throat, like back there, and you don't know whether he did it himself, or whether he got murdered."

Leah nodded. "About the only suicides you can be sure of just by looking is slit wrists. Not that you can't just go up and ask. It's not like people are embarrassed about it or won't tell you."

"Hmm," said Barto. "I've never been much of a going-up-and-asking type of person."

"It's different here," said Leah. A sigh escaped her—it seemed so wearying to explain. The thing was, nothing would *change*, whether it was explained or not explained. "No one takes offense; no one thinks any the less of you. Just like no one plots against you, or gossips or anything. It's restful. It's pointless; everything is pointless, but nothing is a bother, either."

"Come *on*," said King behind her. The string was at full stretch, and so was King's arm. The Miscreant was dragging his feet, his eyes cast fearfully upward.

Leah turned impatiently from the sight. *She* had lived a virtuous life, if a short one. Her only sin was one of omission, and not even *her* omission, but her parents': she was one of the billions of unbaptized who walked the Outer.

The breeze was very warm now, and Leah could smell the sulfur. The smell, the rumbling, and the occasional sprinkle of pumice on her head and into the surrounding grass were the only indications of the sufferings going on overhead. At least she didn't have to worry about finding herself in Hell; her only question was when, if ever, she would be granted admission to that better place.

Mostly Leah didn't get to see much inside Heaven; clerical errors usually went the other way from this one, and Souls delivered to Heaven slipped in quickly, as soon as the Gate opened the merest crack. This time, because the Miscreant had made such a fuss, some force had been needed to remove him, and the Gate had had to be opened comparatively wide. The four members of the escort had been tortured long and hard by the sight of the Eternal Benediction, of that constant rain of powdery shimmer—was it food? was it love?—that fell through the rays of Light, that clung to the clouds, that brushed past the beings. The snatches of music, the humming of crystal, the tang of harp strings, the celestial harmonies sung by voices so human, so joyous—Leah, accustomed only to the whistling breezes in the Outer, to the weeping and mumbling of the Souls Pending, had listened hard and fiercely. She resolved to memorize a single phrase to take with her, to give her heart during the gray times. And she had; she'd caught a little flourish of notes and hammered them into her memory.

But then the Gate had closed and silenced the music, and the Miscreant Soul had stood naked and dismayed before them, subdued by the string but still panting from the fight. Leah had run the caught phrase through her mind several times and it had fallen dead, all its brilliance and mystery and beauty gone, a string of notes as bland and gray-green as the clothes she wore. The four of them, whose pure yearning toward Heaven had fused them elbow to elbow into a single being, had fallen apart, four blockish, clumsy entities excluded into a quieter, grayer eternity. One needed nothing here, not food or drink or love— but a glimpse of Heaven woke a hunger, a hunger *to hunger* again, to long for something, anything, and have that longing satisfied, to feel any feeling but this bland resignation, this hopeless doggedness, this pointless processing of oneself forward through unmarked, unmemorable time. Oh, and then the hunger went, and left you frowning, trying to fathom how you could have felt as strongly as that about anything.

Walking through the grasslands was tedious now; Leah's shins stung with grass cuts. There were few Souls here, either floating or walking, and they kept their distance—if you weren't a Shepherd, no one was interested in you. A few children stood and stared, head and shoulders above the grasses, but anyone in their teens or older hunched and turned and swayed slowly away as the escort came through on its business.

The rumbling overhead became louder; the shell of the sphere was thinner the closer they approached Hell's Gate.

"I can hear people screaming, I think," whimpered the Miscreant.

"Not yet," said King. "You're imagining it."

"Put another loop around his neck if he's feeling resistant," said Tabatha. "That'll keep him moving."

They paused while King arranged this, Tabatha instructing him. "You want it firm, but not tight, and you don't want it to get any tighter when you pull on it, just like the first one."

The grass clumps grew farther apart now, and the ground between was bare and red, uneven and littered with sharp stones. It was quite hard to keep an even pace, and the whole team slowed, picking places to put their feet. The stones grew bigger and bigger, broader and more treacherously balanced.

"This is like gibber plain," said Barto. "I remember when we went on our round-Australia trip. Except there'd be no creatures here. We looked through these binoculars that could see infrared light and there were all sorts of things—little mice jumping around, lizards, spiders. . . ."

No one answered. Leah had barely understood him. Gibber?

Australia? Binoculars? Infrared? And she wasn't going to reiterate, *No, there are no animals here. Animals are old-world stuff; they just circulate in that system.* And then he'd ask, *So why are there plants here—aren't they old-world, too? I don't know,* she'd have to say. *Did I create this? If you ever get to Heaven, I'm sure it'll all be made clear.* It was all too boring and took too much energy.

A frail tower of scaffolding appeared on the horizon, leading up to Hell's lowest convexity. The escort picked their way toward it, swearing under their breath as the stones bit into their feet, staggering off balance now and again. The Miscreant fell once, opening a cut on his forehead and bruising his cheek.

"I couldn't put my hands out," he complained. "Maybe you could just untie my hands for this part?"

"I'm sorry." King brushed the red dust off the man's belly, genitals, and thigh. "We'll just walk a bit slower, shall we?"

"You know," said the Miscreant, "it's almost good to feel pain! The pain is better than the nothingness, don't you think? What a terrible place this is! Do you get a lot of people purposely hurting themselves here?"

"When they first arrive, sometimes," said Tabatha. "But they calm down after a while and fit in with the rest of us."

Leah watched the red ground pass. Tabatha was a bit of a goody-goody, she thought. *The rest of us*—how cozy. What a cozy little community we are.

"After all, you can't end this yourself," Tabatha went on. "You can't self-harm your way out of it. Only way out is to pick up brownie points, or by intercession from someone back in the old world."

Brownie points, was it? Leah wondered what the All Mighty would think of that phrase.

Wooden stairs zigzagged up inside the scaffolding. The canvas enclosing its middle two sections rippled in the breeze. "Up we go, then." Tabatha started to climb.

Leah brought up the rear. She hung back a little so as to have the Miscreant's grubby feet at her eye level, rather than his flabby white bottom and bitten-nailed hands.

In the first canvas room they took woven booties from the water trough and tied them to their feet. Water squeezed from the thick soles and rained between the floorboards onto the steps below. They slopped upstairs to the second room.

"This is where we turn over," King told the Miscreant. "Don't freak out—it might feel a bit weird."

"Whee," said Tabatha, somersaulting off the top step into the shadows.

"You out of the way?" Barto jumped after her.

"It's quite enjoyable." King turned in the opening and addressed the Miscreant upside down. "It's about the most fun anyone gets in this place."

The Miscreant's boots lifted off the step. "No, wait a minute—" He kicked out, and water flew into Leah's face. He misjudged everything; his head banged on the top step. His frightened, wounded face stared out at Leah for a moment before he floated up into the dim landing space.

"Christ, King, you're supposed to be looking after him." Leah's hair rose and the weight lifted out of her spine. She checked the air above and let go into it. Bodies revolved in the dim tented space, and water drops wobbled, unsure which way to fall. "Let's move along now," she said.

They bounced and sprang along the weightless landing to the far door and dropped out onto the upper stairs. Now the creased, pockmarked gray rock of the Hell sphere was the ground, and the sky that hung over them was the red stony plain. The air was close and smelly.

Down they went onto the rock. Their boots hissed on contact with it.

"Not far now," said Tabatha.

"I don't care how far it is," muttered the Miscreant.

Leah peered around him at the machinery and the desk in the distance, and the staffers moving about getting ready for them.

Tsss, tsss, tsss, tsss, went the booties for the first little while. Then the soles dried out, and the smell of charred grass began to join that of sulfur. It was uncomfortably hot. The ground was creased cooled lava, easier to walk on than stones or swamp.

"Pick up the pace," said King to the Miscreant, "or our boots'll run out on the way back."

"Oh, poor you," said the Miscreant, obediently starting to jog. "How you'll suffer."

As if you had cause to complain, thought Leah. *It's not as if you weren't warned. Everybody gets warned somehow, even if they're brought up under a Wrong God. Oog*—she made herself look away from his jogging bottom—*so much flesh. If I'd grown that old, I never would've let that happen to me.*

"Ahoy there," cried a woman in a silver fire suit up ahead, clapping her gloved hands. "You got a Clerical there for us?"

"I don't know what he is—that's not my privilege," said Tabatha. "All I know is, he goes in here."

"Good-oh," said a fire-suited man. "Helps us tell one moment from another." He shot Leah a cold grin.

The man at the desk was small, hunched, and pernickety-looking. He took the satchel and peered down his nose at each paper in turn, as if keeping an invisible pair of reading glasses on his nose. Then he dropped his head, glowered at them above the same glasses, and pointed a thumb at the machinery.

Leah had been here twice before. Both times she'd been picking up, and the Soul had been waiting for them, sitting happily on the desk swinging his legs. She'd never seen the machinery operate before.

One of the fire-suited people slapped a switch and the whole black affair shuddered into life. All the staffers had their headpieces on now—they were silver all over, with flat black faces. They each took, from a hook on the machine's slabby side, a silver pole that divided at the top into many vicious little spikes.

The wheels turned. The chain tightened on the eyebolt in the ground. The circle of the lid was suddenly clear in the rock, outlined in knee-high puffs of smoke. Human screams rushed out with the smoke.

The Miscreant leaped back, pulling the string from King's hand. He ran, but Leah dived after him and brought him down by the ankle, and the others piled straight on top of him. Leah jumped up off the scorching ground and pinned his leg down. Barto bucked on the other one and Tabatha and King took care of arms and torso. "It's too *late*. It's too *late*," Tabatha said grimly into the man's ear. "Where do you think you would run to?"

Still he struggled. "Bloody hell," said Barto, almost thrown off the leg. He took a firmer hold. "Strong! Who would've thought such a flabby old thing—"

The Miscreant bucked and rippled again.

"How can he stand it? He must be burning all down his front—"

"You know what will stop this?" Leah hissed at Barto. "Grabbing him by the nuts. Bags you do it."

"Bags I *don't*."

"Go on." This was almost funny. Leah was almost laughing. "You're the boy."

"Eesh, I'm not grabbing some old feller's *nuts*!"

"Here." A fire suit came up. "Move aside," he said in a muffled voice. "I'll pitchfork him."

Gently he lowered his spike points onto the Miscreant's back.

"That's better." Tabatha gingerly climbed off the captive.

They all slid off him. King took up the string again. "Now don't try that again," he said. "This man will happily poke you straight into the fire like a marshmallow on a stick."

They helped the Miscreant up. He was crying now; his front was all red, flecked with black from the ground. His face was terrible, all crumpled and slaver-y like that, and with its injuries.

"Please, please," he said. "Oh no, please!"

He could hardly use his legs. He was extremely heavy. They dragged him toward the lid. It was a little way open now.

Something moved in the smoke like a dark sea anemone. Trying to see it more clearly, Leah felt holes open in the Outer's grayness, which shrank somewhat on her mind, at the touch of a realization, and with the realization, feeling.

For they were hands, all those movements, blood-red hands on the blood-streaked, steaming arms of the Damned. In a frenzy they waved and clutched at the Outer's air; they pawed the lid and the ground; they left prints; they wet and reddened the rock with their slaps and slidings.

The fire suits stood well back from the opening. Any hand that found a grip they prodded until it flinched back into the waving mass, into the high suffering howl of Hell.

The Miscreant pressed back into his escort; Leah couldn't hear him for machine noise and screaming, but she felt the horror as if he were squeezing it out like a sponge, as if she were taking it up like a sponge, a gray, dry sponge soaking up juice and color. Suddenly Barto's face was open, lively; suddenly there was a vigor in Tabatha's bracing herself to push, in King's new grasp on the Miscreant's upper arm. Leah pulled in a great noseful of the dreadful, wonderful cooking-meat smell of the Damned, the hot-metal smell of the machinery, the thick yellow stench of brimstone.

The machinery ground; the massive lid lifted unsteadily, revealing its many layers of black polished rock and brass, all smattered with Damned-fluids. Smoke, some yellow, some gray, some black, belched out all around; steam jetted white across the ground. Coughing, Leah heaved the Miscreant forward by his shoulder.

A Damned Soul sprang out of the smoke. It caught the Miscreant by the shoulder, Leah by her arm, and screamed in their faces in a fast, foreign language. Its eyes rolled and steamed; its whole face was misshapen. The skin of it, the raw skin—

"Git back there!" growled a fire suit, forcing the Soul back with a pole across its middle. Through the smoke and the glorious all-engulfing sensations of her own retching, Leah had an impression of a person being folded and forced away. Like a crab into a crevice, she thought, pushing the Miscreant forward again—only rubbery. And raw—that skin! The points of the pitchfork had sliced across that Soul's belly, and the wounds had *sizzled* with blood and fluids rushing to heal it, to make the skin clean and raw again and ready to suffer more.

This was what she wanted, what she needed, to see such things and to see them clearly. The sulfur jabbed her nostrils and she sniffed it up and coughed, exultant. The Miscreant's shaggy boot toes flamed near the lip of the opening; hands painted them red, stroke by stroke. She took slippery white handfuls of him and, in a spasm of revulsion and joy, forced him into the center of the red sea anemone.

Its many arms hauled him in. Maybe they thought they could pull themselves past him into the Outer; perhaps they thought to plead with him; maybe they just wanted someone else to share their misery. Whatever they wanted, the red Souls folded the white, flailing Soul in.

It was like watching a kebab being rolled, Barto would say later. *A chicken kebab.*

Don't be awful, Tabatha would say, trying to cringe, trying to care enough.

The escort pulled their hands and feet free of the roaring Souls. Pitchforks poked and hissed, intervening for them. The machinery clanked; the lid shuddered and began to lower. In the desperate red scramble just inside the rim, the faces—*I will never forget these*, Leah thought raptly, *I will never be able*—the hairless faces, all melted and remelted flesh, spat and bubbled and ran with juices. And they knew—their eyes begged and their bloodied lips pleaded in a thousand different languages.

Barto gagged beside Leah, King clutched her and wept, Tabatha dragged at their sleeves: "Come away! Come away!"

But Leah stayed, her eyes and heart still feasting. Just as she'd craned for the last possible glimpse of that other eternity, Heaven, so she must peer around the fire suit to see as many hands, as many faces as she could, as the lid crushed them, as they clutched the very pitchforks that forced them back into suffering.

"Bloody, sticky things!" The nearest fire suit scraped off against the rim a Soul that had impaled itself chest-first upon her fork. "How much more pain do you want?" The Soul fish-flopped, then was clawed away by others more desperate, more able.

The dire howling lessened; there were just hands now, flickering among the yellow flames that came up where hopeless Souls had dropped away and left gaps in the crowd. They made a frill, a lacework of red fingers, a fur of black-and-yellow smoke, a feather of gold flame, a stinking sleeve edge that shortened, shortened—

Thud. The lid closed, sealing in the Damned.

The fire suit turned away and snatched off her hood. The

woman inside grinned down at Leah. "Better get a move on," she said.

Tabatha was already starting for the tower, grabbing up the satchel as she passed the desk. Barto stared at the lid over Leah's shoulder, both hands to his mouth. King, on all fours, leaned hard against her knees, retching.

"Come on, laddie." The fire suit prodded him gently with her bloodied pitchfork. "Those boots won't last much longer."

"And you're burning yourself." Leah pulled on his shoulder.

Supporting him, she followed Tabatha. They must take the stamped papers up to Heaven Gate and lodge them. Leah's imagination was as clear as a sunlit tide pool now; she could just see those snooty Registrars dipping their quills to add the marks, the *brownie points,* to each team member's record book. Those marks would build—who knew how fast? who knew how many were needed?—until there were enough to release him or her from the Outer forever, and into Heaven and the Eternal Benediction and the Light.

Leah's feet stung. The soles of the booties were black and fringed with burned strands of rushes.

"Hurry, King." She pushed him along in the small of the back.

He tried to speak over his shoulder—his face was greenish, and his lips puffed out with nauseated burps. "I heard one of them say—"

"Just *run*, King! Talk when we get to the ladder!"

And they ran, pell-mell, elated. One of Barto's booties gave out, shredding off his foot. He tried a strange hopping run for a few paces, then seemed to take off and fly across the hot black ridges to the scaffolding.

They flung themselves after him, finally landing in a clump on the lowest steps. A few moments filled with groans and panting. Then they spread out onto separate steps.

"Oh, my *feet!*"

"Uff! This is from his fingernails, look! Like a—like a *tiger* claw or something."

"Look at King!" King's hands and knees had swelled up as if inflated.

"He whacked me in the mouth *so* hard, that Soul. I thought I'd lost some teeth. I think this one's a bit wobbly. Does this look wobbly to you, Leah?"

When every injury had been noted and admired, quiet descended. The grayness crept in at the edges of Leah's mind.

King pushed his face into the hot breeze. "I heard someone say, 'It's so cool out there!'"

"I heard that, too," said Tabatha quietly.

"I heard someone call out, 'Water, water!'" whispered Barto. "And you know? For just that moment, I was thirsty."

Leah's tongue searched her mouth for that feeling. No, she wasn't thirsty, not even after all that heat and smoke and running.

"I didn't understand anything they said." She spoke quickly, while there was still a bit of space in the middle of the encroaching grayness. "But what I *saw* . . ." She tried to remember that screaming Soul's face well enough to make her stomach churn again. She rubbed her tearless eyes, and saw against the lids a vague bobbing of bald, red heads, waving hands, silent mouths. Nothing that would upset anybody. "Aagh." The grayness reached the center of her feelings and winked them out.

That was all she would be left with, until next time—that bobbing impression, all the intensity faded to a thin gray knowledge, a small, puzzled struggle to remember. What had been so wonderful?

Tabatha was binding Barto's foot with a strip torn off her uniform. "We must move in and out quicker next time," she said absently. "Like a pickup. This never would've happened with a pickup."

"How do they get them out of there, with a pickup?" wondered King. "Without anyone else escaping?"

"If you ever get to work there, I guess you'll find out," said Tabatha flatly.

"You can't blame us for being curious," said King. He must have not quite recovered, thought Leah.

Anyway, *curious* wasn't the word for it. She followed the others up the stairs, rolled over and dropped into the Outer's gravitational field, followed them through the bootie room and down onto the stony red plain. Curiosity was a lame, small-scale thing. What it was, was . . .

She picked her way through the stones toward the lighter regions of the Outer. She tried to think, to search what she thought was her heart. But she was not let see. The Outer's grayness had her; it walled the thought she was reaching for in fog, embedded the feeling in cloud; it clumsied her toes and fingers and all her finer faculties and left her with only this, the barest inclination to keep moving, in the direction that felt like forward, but might turn out never to be forward, or backward, or any way, anywhere, ever.

Mouse Maker

"Who started this?" Bet struggled with the women holding her down. "That Topsy Strongarm, I'll be bound! She's been looking for her chance."

"Let's shut up that noise, for a start," said Pater Bill, and they stuffed one cloth in her mouth and tied another round it.

At least, that is what Darby says. I wasn't there myself. I would have none of it. It had all happened without me. Honestly, I said not a word to anyone about what I had heard nor seen. But these things get known, gossip or not. However quiet you keep, matters like this, they come out some way.

She lives not far from me, Bet Cransk. The land is arranged so she must walk along my fence line, in my field, to get to her own place from the road. I am used to her, and maybe people would have left her alone if they had been used to her, too. Because most of the time she is harmless, if noisy when you get her going.

"And handy," Dan's widow said when she was being friendly, when she was thinking maybe she could like me for the sake of picking up my land as well as Dan's. "It don't hurt to have a salve woman up your own hill, that you can run to in fever or tummy rack."

Which was also true, though I only ever used Bet for that bad sickle wound I made in my leg, and the one evening where she told my fortune. And a solid fortune it will be. I don't know how I'm to get to it from here, exactly, but there it is.

There it is, she said. *It's in the cards and it's in the cup and it's in that oil-and-ink. If all three say it, it's gold and good opinion all the way for you, Pedder.*

We laughed at that, sitting in her grubby house that is more burrowed than built into the bank there. Even her dandy-wine was dirty, sediment shifting in it like white smoke. Her cards were so filthy I could barely see the signs on them.

Taking against the mayor was her error. Well, really, she was against the whole town council in the end; well, really, the whole town. But she got it fixed in her head that Pater Mears was the one with the set against her, so she was loudest against him.

"It's only a scare," I said. "Just wait. Be cunning," I said. "Leave your cards at home a few times; tell in other ways. People still want to know. Some will even come up here, if they want the cards. Laurel Whistler, for one. I don't mind her using the way."

But Bet was fretting, there on my doorstep. "The cards is the best," she said. "The cards is what everyone wants. The cards is what people pay for."

"Well, the cards is what gives people the wobbles, too," I said testily; how long had I been standing there saying and saying?

"Bylaws!" She spat a big white spit on my path. "Coming at me with his papers. *This here,* he says, *it's my seal, look at it. It means you have to stop with the weeds and the divination, or I'll have you put in the roundhouse a week or two. It's law now,* he said— smug pottlehead—*here in this writing.* I told him—Jollyon Mears, young enough to be my granson! I told him he could put his big red mayor's seal in his big red—"

"You want to be careful," I said. She had already told me all this. "They can do what they say, however young they are."

"They're a bunch of scheming souses, taking away a widow's honest living while they guzzle and chomp in the meeting-house!"

"Maybe so," I said. I was tired. I had been plowing all day while she was off squabbling. I had just sat down to my bread and tea when she arrived. "But you don't want to get on their wrong side, either."

The widow thing—I don't know even if it was true, though she always brought it up when she wanted sympathy. It was well before my time, and no one could tell me who the lucky gentle-man had been—but no one could exactly say she hadn't had him, either. She is not a solid citizen, that you can feel sure of. There's always this cloud of uncertainties around her, like mist or flies. Some of the time I like that, when the solid citizens are getting up my nose; some of the time it gives me the jinks just as badly as it does everyone else.

Pater Bill had his beadle stick, Darby says, and he laid the first blow. Which was all the others needed. Women they were, mostly dealing as they must with a woman; they wanted the beadle's authority to begin, but once he gave it, he might as well have left Bet's house right then for all the chance he got at her.

"It wasn't like they wanted to kill her," says Darb. "They just wanted to teach her a lesson."

"In which case why they went for her head is mysterious to me," I said to him. "Why they knocked her senseless so that she could not *hear* their lesson, hmm?"

Darby was quiet.

"And why they kept hitting when she was down and had long ceased to fight them?"

Darby pulled at a scrap of loose skin by his fingernail.

"They should have put her in the prison," I said.

"They could prove nothing," said Darby. "It was all rumor and old history and the word of Sarah Slattly and—"

"Not for punishment," I said. "For protection."

At first it was only rushings in the night, very like wind or a passing patter of rain. It was only later on that they woke me properly and made me wonder, later when the damage became clear and it looked like we might all bloody starve. That's them now, I thought. They're running past my door. And they've been coming and coming, a run of them every short while, regular all night, regular every fine night this last while. And I got myself up and when I judged the time to be right I opened my door on the moonlight and stood there wrapped in my blanket and waiting.

And there they came, all running together in a pack, so tiny and yet so many that all their little toenails scraping, all their little paws hitting, made that sound upon the ground, that whisper like wind or rain. They ran so close together they were like a stretch of moss that pulled itself up and went hurrying off. They gleamed with good health and with eyes in the moonlight. I stood on my step and they ran along the front of my house and some fetched up and swirled against the step and some ran across and around my feet. But none ran in my door; every one passed on. They ran straight through my small crop without climbing a single stalk. I saw them flow through like water and be gone.

It was a cold night and, as I said, fine. I walked out onto my path in my blanket and the moonlight was silver all around me, throwing down hard black shadows, their edges fine as a butcher knife's. Up the hill where the mice had come from, a wisp of smoke floated up over Bet Cransk's place, and I couldn't say I was surprised.

I could have protected her. I could have stood up and spoken for her. I'm not small. I'm not the most respected man, I'm no pater, but neither am I no one; I am not of no account.

I could at least have given them pause. A better neighbor might have been there and said something, made them think what they were doing.

She was stupid about it; she was obvious. The damage started at Binder's Copse and never a step east of it. You could see the line in Binder's crop, wriggling gray one side, golden and straight the other. And everyone knew, from all his battles, how the town boundary ran across Binder's land. Didn't I go cold, standing there with mice patting the toes of my boots, but not the heels! I could have stepped from clear road into the carpet of them and back out again; they drew the boundary with their bodies.

So once the council saw that, they only had to look for someone with a grievance against them, didn't they? Someone with a grievance and with no authority except over such as this, except over mice and such.

I did what I could for her, though I barely recognized her. They have not broken her skull. I shouldn't think she will die. But they shook up her brain in its box fairly fiercely; she has not made much sense since. And who would have thought a head could look so softened, bulging and bleeding and all miscolored, as if it had been baked wrong? Her beaten eyes, believe it, are bigger than her mashed nose. You can hear the hard work it is, moving the breath in and out of that face. You can *smell* the blood that won't be sopped up out of the earthen floor, however hard I press the cloth to it.

Perhaps it was the smell that made me decide to cook—to

cover it. More likely it was the moon, which makes all sorts of madness in a person, turns everything into a dream. And I was alone up here, with the town's rage written into Bet's face, and my own anger, my own bad conscience, passing through me wave on wave at the sight of her, regular like the mice, keeping me from dozing. Keeping me even from sitting; I threw myself up off the bench and paced about and sought for breath out in the silvery air.

Finally all those things preyed on me enough: the black canister on the shelf, the heap of shavings next to it, the little slabs of bark, the herbs. Serve them right, I thought. Give them the lie if it works. Or some such thinking. I don't remember. I was eager to try it; that is the truth.

Last moon I came up here, you see. I had lain and lain in my bed and looked up at the shadows in the roof, and every now and again the little rushing passed my door, pitter-patter, like a handful of grain cast across the hard ground there, across the step. I knew she could not get away with it much longer. *I* would burst and tell soon, if someone else did not.

Bootless and in my nightshirt I went up, as if pretending to myself I was not really going anywhere, not really leaving my home.

I sat out in the dark on a stump and watched her through her open door. Bare-armed and red-faced she was, and busy. She steamed up the water on her fire outside, and then she hurried it to the table and put all the things in, always in the same order, always in the same amounts. And she stirred it and she put the lid on and she held her breath three times as long as she could, and she lifted off the lid again.

And *fluffuther-fluffuther* over the rim they came like boiling, only the boilings ran away on little gray-and-pink legs, and pulled gray tails behind them. They poured off the table edges and ran out the door and away to the west, to the town. And Bet came out once more and filled the empty pot from the water butt.

I sat there in the dark and watched, again and again. It was a dance, and by dawn I had picked up the rhythm of it, and I knew all the steps.

Many's the time I would pass Bet on the road, going slowly along and looking, some skinny white root with earth still on it in one hand, some bunch of pulled greeneries in the other.

"Hey, Bet. What you up to there?"

"Pedder."

"What you hunting?"

"Bits and bobbles," she always said. "What is good to eat and good to medicine people."

Mater Strongarm maintained she saw Bet gathering in the graveyard, of a full moon or a new. But then, you got to ask what the mater herself was doing wandering that side of town in the night. And you've got to remember, this is a woman who considered selling her own daughter to Travelers, that hard winter that nearly never ended. Mater Strongarm would do a lot for coin or her own advantage. I myself think Bet didn't wish anyone evil that didn't deserve it.

I put the pot on to boil. I ready everything on the table, the table that is usually such a clutter, but which the paters and maters so kindly cleared with their sticks when they came here to do their punishment. I put the things all in a row in the order I saw Bet use them. I open the canister ready. It is heavy, half full of black grains. I stand there stuck, my finger in the canister's mouth. I want to reach in and stir the grains, to know how they feel, to see if they crumble. But something will not let me.

I put canister and lid on the table. I go out and sit on the stump where I watched before. I almost drop with exhaustion there—suddenly sleep is on me, pressing down inside my face. But then the pot lid clanks and I'm up and collecting it, ready to do the dance.

And dance I do. *Rustle* go the lamb leaves, *crackle* go the bay, *plop* goes the bark, and the two pinches of black grains turn the whole to murk. The paper and the shriveled thing, the snip of man-drag root, the wood shaving and four of the berries. All done, so I pick up the spoon, which is mouse-colored with this use, and seven times stir one way and seven times the other, just like Bet did the night I watched her.

Then I clap the lid on and hold my breath. Bet Cransk's sleeping face watches, warped as some clumsy, child-made mask, all its puffs and pillows shining in the candlelight.

After the third breath, off I lift the lid, triumphant, eager for the fountain of mice.

Nothing.

Not quite nothing. The water's still there, still hot. Hot and empty and clear. All the stuffs I put in it are gone. Wasted, I think. All gone to make a pot of empty water.

I'm about to put the lid back on, to carry the pot to the door and empty the magicked water down the hill. Then I see it.

"Hah!"

It's at the bottom on the near side, crawling slowly along the near side.

I reach for the spoon. "I've made *one*, at least."

I lift it out and put it on the table, and bring the candle near.

Eugh. It's an abomination of a mouse. It has all the elements, but they have come together wrong, all in the wrong places. Pieces that should be inside are outside and dragging, leaving wet marks on the table. One of the eyes is about right, but the other shines out from the back, near the root of the crooked half tail. There are only three legs. And the whole skin—there is scarcely any hair on the thing—is wrong, shriveled, boiled, painful-looking. The whole mouse is suffering, the way it shudders and creeps, the way its mouth works in its side there, as if it is trying to scream.

It's easy to kill a mouse. Jeesh, hasn't the whole town been stomping and smearing them underfoot these last months? Doesn't everyone up to the oldest and down to toddlers know the exact force needed to pop out the life of one and not have it stick to your boot and smell there?

I know I will wish I hadn't killed it quite so fast, hadn't taken it by its tail stump and thrown it with such force and so far in among the trees. I'll want to take another look at it, to see again exactly where its parts are, exactly how it moves, to think about what I made and wonder that I made it, however monstrous it is, that I cooked up a thing that lived, in however much pain.

But while it shudders there and looks in two directions and makes that sticky sound in its mouth, the only thing to do is smack it out of life with the spoon, then cast it away where no one will ever see it again. I stand at the forest edge, wiping my hands down my shirt, over and over, to rid them of the touch of the tail. I hurry into Bet's house, pick up the water pot, busily empty and rinse it. I must forget that I even saw the mouse-thing, let alone that I boiled it up myself out of Bet's bits and bobbles. I must put it out of my mind, completely and forever, the knowledge that I could do such a thing. For where would that lead? What good could it bring me?

Forever Upward

As soon as I saw it, I knew. That was my first time, then, but I didn't stop to make sure. Today was the last day we could do anything about it, and the sun was already high. So I ran.

"Oh, Valla and Brava and their lazy bums!"

Because it was their chores and their it's-our-last-day-we-don't-care-if-the-pig-starves-it-won't-squeal-until-tomorrow that had slowed me getting up to the lookout.

I thumped from step to step. My little dog, Liklik, skittered down the damp path behind me. I sprang over roots and I swung on the vine over the boggy patch and tied it quickly behind me. Liklik splashed through below. Around us the forest quietened, its dawn musics and battles finished, the sun leaning on the treetops. Two birds whooped to each other from a northern perch and a southern one.

I slid down the broken path past Widow Split's garden patch, dodged through the palm grove there, and shot out among the huts like an arrow. "Mummarn! Mummarn!"

"She is headed down the lagoon," said Brava from the hammock.

"What!"

"For to beat out our bedding." Valla's head popped up at the other end of the hammock. "To wash all trace of us away," he added gloomily.

"But she mustn't!"

"Well, she has." Valla sank back.

"I'll go after her." I waited, hoping one of them would offer his long legs, but of course no. "Did she go long?"

"I wouldn't say long, would you, Brava?"

"Oh, a good while, I'd say."

"Nooo, no more 'an a cock's crow ago." And Valla crowed. "Yes, about that long."

"No, I'd say a good long spell. Long enough to roast that rooster."

"Oh, I'll be so *glad* when that Church takes you!" I burst out as I ran from them. It wasn't true, but it *felt* true just at that moment. "Come, Lik!"

My brothers' laughter followed us down into the forest.

This is the way it had been once: all the gods we needed—of fish, fruit, feather, fur, grain, and weather, of water salt and sweet—we had found and tamed so that we wanted for nothing.

Then the Church came. I don't remember that day; I was too little, and Mummarn says she put her hand over my eyes so

131

that I would not see. They broke our stone ancestors and took away the pieces; they burned our wooden ones. Mummarn took us into the forest. *But we could still smell the burning*, she says.

They burned all the guardians; they defiled all the summoning places so that the gods would not come to them. *You don't need these*, they said. *You've got the one true god now who looks after everything.* As if a single god could swell fruit on a tree *and* set water springing *and* bring a school of silver-mask over the sandbar for us!

As if a god would be shaped like that, said the widows when you got them going, *just like a man, forked and bearded with a mouth no wider than a spear hole! How can he be one true, and be so small?*

Of our men, all I remembered was that they had smelled strong and taken up most of the space. When the first big rains came after the Church took them, the lunghouse was barely half full. It felt wonderful to me—there was room to play without running into people. But all the widows wept. *How can they say their god is kind*, they said, *when he is a man only, and only allows men near him? What sort of god cuts a family down the middle like a carcass, and leaves the women husband- and sonless, and the children fatherless in the forest? They should cut out our hearts and turn them on spits before our eyes—that would hurt less!*

Back and forth down the slope I went with Liklik, through the mud and dimness under the ferns. When we were out of my brothers' hearing I called again, "Mummarn!" over and over.

Finally a tiny voice called back, well below me: "Is that you, Currija?"

"Mummarn, come back!" I hurried on.

At last there she was, with the rolled bed mats on her back pointing up behind her head like a meander-bird's crest, and her dog, Charger, at her heel. She was as shiny with sweat as the rock beside her was shiny with water weeping out of the ground. She held her head steady under the pot of soap leaves and scrub brushes—only her eyes tilted to me. "What is it, daughter?"

"I saw it! The bait! The house on a string! From the lookout!"

She gave such a start, she had to put her hands up to the pot. What a look came onto her face! If she hadn't been so laden, she would have run up and grabbed me.

"This is not some joke idea of your brothers'," she said fiercely.

"No, Mummarn! It's just as you said: a pearly-white house, with a smaller house on top. I even saw the string; sunlight went along it. Out over Pinnacle Cliff, it was going, out over the sea!"

"You are sure, absolutely? Because there is no time for me to check. We must snatch up our offerings and *run!*" She started up toward me with big steps.

"I am sure! It could not be anything else! It was certainly not a cloud."

"A sea eagle?" Her eyes had come up level with mine, still fierce, still doubting me.

"Absolutely could not be an eagle. It had a lo-ong tail, like a flag, as you said. . . ." With my arm I tried to show her the way the tail had rippled, slowly, its full length.

She watched my arm. Wonderment cleared the fierceness from her face. "Here. Take this." She pushed the pot into my hands. "Gods help us, is it too late?"

I scampered up the path after her muddy heels and the dogs' curled, muddy tails. What were we going to see? What would we do? All I knew was to check for the house every morning, and that there was hope in seeing it. What came after, I could only guess.

My brothers' heads popped up as we hurried inside.

"What's happening?" called Brava.

"Don't tell them," said Mummarn, taking the cloths off the glory basket. "Tie up the dogs. They can't come with us."

"Mummarn?" said Valla.

"Nothing. None of your business, big boys."

"Ah, what? Tell us!"

She pushed two little skins at me. "Fill."

When I came back, the boys were still complaining, but Mummarn was silent, tying a bundle. "Get us some of those baby bulbs that we can eat raw," she muttered to me.

So I went out and withstood the whining as I dug.

"What *is* it? What is so secret? Is it a present for us?"

"It's the one thing that's *not* for you," said Mummarn from inside. She didn't raise her voice, but they heard it and went silent. "It's for me and Currija."

"You're going away from us?" Valla sat up straighter and watched me. Valla was the quick one. "On our last day?" His voice wobbled a little.

"I cannot choose the day," said Mummarn, clacking kitchen jars.

I knocked the worst dirt off the bulbs and gathered them into my shirt. Mummarn met me at the door, the tied bundle in

134

one hand, the loose one of waterskins and foodstuffs in the other. She eyed Valla over me as I packed the bulbs and tied the bundle.

He was still playing the sad look—no, he really *was* sad all of a sudden. He wasn't pretending.

She went and hugged him, violently, and kissed him in that stinging, deafening way she had.

"Aargh! Mummarn!" he laughed, and Brava fought her off, too, when she came at him. Liklik barked on the end of his cord. Charger watched disapprovingly.

"Go, go!" said Brava. "Go where you have to go! Just don't kiss me!"

We went away laughing, and then we were serious and hurrying, all the way down to the beach. *Just for me and Currija*—I was glad to have heard her say that; I was so glad to be hurrying along with her, because for so long now it had been all about the boys, and spoiling and serving them while we still could. Really, I did not want them to go—who would make Mummarn laugh when Brava was not here? who would shoo my bad dreams away when Valla was gone?—but having them here was no good, either. Nowadays they upset everybody; some of the widows wept just looking at them.

When we reached the flat, Mummarn rushed ahead of me out of the trees. I followed at my same pace. The house was tiny in the sky. Mummarn wept and stamped about in the soft sand.

"Give me your bundle," I said, trying to sound sensible.

She released it to me. Now she had both arms to wave, both hands to catch the tears that were spilling out.

135

"Mummarn? We must hurry." I didn't like her like this; I liked her closed-lipped and watchful, taking care of us.

She took my head in her wet hands and cried hard into my hair. "My only daughter," she wept. "My only child." The sun stung my shoulders. Her tears fell on me and the breeze cooled the stripes they made.

She took back the bundle of offering and struck off toward the harder sand, where it was easier to walk. She sobbed loudly, freely. She staggered with the crying; sometimes she blindly crossed shallows, soaking the edge of her skirt, her face in her free hand.

As we walked, the high cliffs moved across and hid the pale construction in the sky. The beach narrowed, and we climbed up to the path-marker rock and were back in forest.

Mummarn had less breath to cry with as the path steepened; eventually she stopped altogether. We paused at the spring to refill our waterskins; the rest of the morning we climbed. I thought my knees would break from all their bending; my eyes wearied of the steep brown dirt and white roots of the path. Hunger chewed on the inside of me like a dog on an old bone. But the sun would not let us rest and eat; it would not slow, but climbed ever upward—just like us, only so much faster and farther. Every time I checked where it was, my stomach clenched nervously and I tried to hurry.

At last we reached the tufty top of Pinnacle Cliff. The sunlight blasted down, and the breeze was only a fitful thing in the green and purple needle grasses. I stood at the edge of the tree cover and swayed with tiredness.

Mummarn had brought me here once before, more leisurely, to show me the frame fixed into the rock. Now a wooden reel sat in that frame, just as she had told it, with a single loop of strong white twine knotted around it. The twine arced away into the blue; sometimes there was the white speck of the house out there at the end of it, sometimes there was nothing. The reel, the frame, the clifftop, my very bones, thrummed with the wind that the house gathered at the horizon and brought to us along the string.

A woman sat on a mat under a shade cloth, facing out to sea and sky.

"Greetings!" Mummarn called out.

The woman turned. She didn't greet us back, and her face didn't change. She stood and took off her shawl. She was big and hale. Her flat breasts hung nearly to the top of her skirt and were fastened against her body with a woven band.

She came to us. Mummarn gave her two big pearls and a bluestone club. The woman put these under her sitting mat. She unlashed the reel's handle from the frame and began to wind in the twine.

Mummarn led me to the shade cloth. We sat on the matting and divided our food into three, leaving a third for the winding-woman. Then we ate every bulb and dumpling, every scrap of the meat of our shares. When we had finished I felt not so dizzy, not so liable to stagger off the cliff by mistake. "Ah, I needed that." I tied the bones up in the cloth to take back to Charger and Liklik.

The woman wound; the shape at the end of the twine

steered slowly toward us. Mummarn started crying again, quietly. I wrapped my arms and legs around her.

At first I thought the house had grown larger, unfolded or exploded from the strain of the wind. But then—I held Mummarn tighter, and she cried harder, as if I were squeezing the tears out of her—I saw that this was not the pearly-coated paper on the whipwood frame that had been loosed into the sky this morning for the first time since Mummarn started me watching many months ago. This was something else completely.

"So beautiful!" said Mummarn, clearing her eyes of tears again.

"It's so bright, it hurts to look." It grew and grew. I was afraid of it. I tried instead to watch the muscles of the winding-woman's back, but the thing on the line pulled my eyes back to it, growing toward us and shining.

It was bigger than all our village buildings together, including the lunghouse. Thick-bodied, it was, special-fleshed to live in the heights of the sky. It was a giant white fish, but it had less shape than a fish; it was a huge worm, but hollow, and more complicated. Its head was all mouth, open and drinking in air. Long fins streamed from its body, striped like a fan-fish's, and it was these, blown against the creature's flesh, then freeing themselves to catch the wind, that made its coming-and-going song, on many notes like a chorus of widows' voices.

"It's just like Widow Hogtie's bags," I whispered to Mummarn. "Those bags she weaves, that she won't let us use for carrying."

"And now you see why," said Mummarn. She took up her offering bundle, and I let go of her except for one fold of her skirt cloth.

The winding-woman looked small now, dark and compact and thick-muscled against the thing's glow. She wound more slowly. The clifftop grass bent and flattened beneath the settling creature. The wind rushed in the mouth. The body was a shining hall, white and the tiniest bit pink, ribbed like the roof of a mouth, or of a lunghouse.

"But it's cleaner," I said. "And thinner. Widow Hogtie's bags are all hoary and scabby and baggy beside this."

The woman went about, tossing ropes over the creature, tying them to wooden pegs in the grasses.

"Look how wide of the god she has to go, to reach those posts," said Mummarn. "Look how much rope is left over. What have we come to? It's hardly more than bait itself."

Now the winding-woman hammered two bentwood brackets into the earth through the creature's lip. Now she stepped into the mouth, and brought out an armful of white-streaked jelly-flesh such as the fins were made of, and spread it out on the grass to make a glossy mat over the flattened lip and into the interior. Now she stood aside and looked at us with her imperturbable face.

I had never stepped inside a landed god before. It is not like walking into an ordinary house, or even into an ordinary whale. But it is how I found out what I was. Entering that hall was the first step to my becoming.

It was cold in there, as cold as the deepest sea to which I

have ever dived. Colder. The flesh we walked on, the streaked, finny jelly-flesh, was cold, and the breath that moved over it filled and chilled everything inside.

It was hooked just like a fish, the twine pressed into its lip, the hook buried in its cheek, running with pink water. But it didn't gasp and throw itself about, not at all.

We walked right in, with care and slowly, stepping over bands of cartilage. My feet sank a little in the aching-cold, cushiony flesh. All my tiredness went from me. All my *life*, my small life, was blown clean out of me by the god's breath, and I walked along as empty as a shell on the beach with the wind whistling through it.

Deep inside, in a small, padded room where the light was dimmer and more purple, we found the house. The god's digestion had crushed it flat and round, its surface creased, shiny like pearl shell with splinters of whipwood pressed into it. It sat half buried in the floor-flesh like an altar stone in a mound of earth.

I tucked myself out of the worst of the wind, against the wall next to the round doorway. Mummarn went forward and crouched beside the altar. She untied her bundle and took out two little drawstring leather bags. She laid them on the house-altar and sat back on her haunches.

"I never thought this day would come!" she said. "The day of my last hope, and all that will come to hear me is some tiddler, dragged in on a baited string. Times were, my grandmother would call your elders out of the sea depths or the sky heights, and they would crowd like schools of fish and flocks of birds, turning and singing at her command."

Mummarn spat angrily, and the floor flinched under her spittle. Out over the sea the god's tail end snapped in the wind, and its body boomed around us. I pressed myself into the cold wall padding. All I had ever done before today was play, and do the bidding of my Mummarn, or my brothers, or whatever widow was near. The only creatures I ever commanded were the dogs, and Valla had taught me that. I had never learned anything by myself; I had never taught myself anything.

But now . . . now I knew. My bones knew; my hands, spread into the damp wall, knew, and the cold, sunken back of my head. How did I know and Mummarn *not* know? How could I be so little and yet so sure that this was not the way, that she was going about it all wrong?

Mummarn went on, "We must make do, I suppose, with this baby god, with this forced messenger. You're all we have. This is my daughter, Currija, and we've come because tonight the pallor-men are coming, and they will take away our last menfolk, my baby boys Valla and Brava, to make Church-men of them. Here in this bag are Brava's hair and nail cuttings, burned and the ashes consecrated according to the old rites, as near as possible. This bag holds Valla's. And here are the boys themselves."

She laid on the altar two little grass dolls with staring stone eyes and shell mouths. It was the first time I had ever seen such figures.

"Keep them safe and stop them forgetting. Tell your elders that's what I want. If they ever come back and can't speak to their mother or their sister in their own tongue; if they ever turn their nose up at a good meal of bulb and lily root and sweet white fish; if they look up in the sky at night and see only that one-true nonsense instead of all our gods painted there in white dots, as clear as clear, the way I've shown them, I will have something to say about it. I will want answers from you, do you hear?"

A wave thundered into the cliff base; I felt it in my feet and in the flesh around me. The dolls stared up into the noise. Some of this was right. The dolls were right, and the bags; I felt that the words of her prayer, they followed the right kind of pattern. But they were not said, they were not *sung*, in a way that this thing would hear them. You only had to listen to the streaming finny music, to the throaty rushing all about us sucking the warmth from our bodies, to know that. The words had to be made part of the song already there, not tossed like so many pebbles at a target, some missing, some hitting. It was amazing to me that Mummarn would be so careless. And I was frightened to find, inside my body—which was only for playing and running and fetching things, after all—this cold-minded person who *just knew*.

"And this," said Mummarn. "You know I'm already angry about this one. I was angry last time, remember? And now I'm sending my sons after him—almost as if you weren't there! Whose business can be so much more important? These are the people of my heart and blood!" And she laid down a bigger doll, with tattoos sewn in pale fibers around his shell mouth and across his chest.

"This one, Arrowman, he's so long gone, I hardly remember

even what he looks like. If a grass doll walked into my house with these tattoos, I'd think it was Arrowman; I'd run up and embrace him—"

She pressed her thumb to one eye, her finger to the other. Tears squeezed out and rolled down.

She wiped her face on her hand and her hand on her skirt. "I know you must be so busy, because the work of a lot of the other gods has fallen to you. You used to only have to look after old sad widows, the people who lived in caves and hermit huts. You used to have a quiet life.

"But look at me! Do you think I'm lying in a hammock drinking nectar all day? I'm trying to be the man as well as the mother of our house. I'm running around the village, getting as much men's business out of all our brains, so that I can tell my sons. I'm making Widow Smite teach them all the fighting she used to know—and getting *her* out of her hammock is a day's work just for one. We've all got to take on extra, with what happened; you can't expect to have it as easy as before."

She was trying to bargain with it? How could she think that *that* would work? How did she think her own doings had anything to do with this thing's sky-life? There was no way to sing what she was saying so that it would matter to any god.

She rearranged my father into the middle of the altar, Valla and his bag on one side and Brava and his on the other.

"Last of all, this is not an offering but an introduction. My daughter, Currija, here, she's coming up to full womanhood soon. I don't know what will be left to her but childless solitude if you don't act soon, but what I'm saying is, I want you to listen to her. She's blameless; she's always done everything right, the way she was told. There's nothing in her to offend you gods, so you take heed of her and stand by her. Whenever she sees this house, she'll come and make offering just like today, and you listen. She's a sensible girl; she knows what needs doing; she'll tell you right."

The singing wavered with the wind, then was steady again. The god was not listening; it had not heard. It was very young and wild; it hadn't a single scar on it. It did not even know we were here.

Mummarn waved me forward. *No, you're wrong,* I almost said. *We don't stand in the middle and throw pebble-words; we press ourselves into the walls, and listen, and sing.* But she looked so tired and cross with me and, as I said, all I had ever done before was obey her.

We stood like totem posts on the soft, unsteady floor. She made me raise my arms like her.

"All my words and offerings," she said loudly, "please take them up into the sky. Put them before all the gods' eyes, pour them into their ears. Move or stay your hands as I've asked, in the name of these following ancients, which I and Currija will recite together."

She nodded to me, and we began. It was clumsy and fruitless; the words fell dead against the walls, when all around us was the rushing breath, any note of which we might have used, and also, outside that noise, the softer singing of the fins, in which we might have tangled our pleas. I closed my eyes and tried to slow down Mummarn's gabbling with my own chant, tried to sneak a little song into the sound.

She slapped my upstretched hand with hers. But just before she did, the god heard me. The god's attention fluttered toward me, cold as cold, there as quick as a stroke of lightning, then gone again with her slap. And huge! What concerns! For the sky, it looks like a flat shell, with sun and moon and stars crawling across its blue or its blackness, but in fact it goes on and on, forever upward the way some parts of the sea go forever down. I knew I was right in my singing, I knew I had done the right thing; still, I was glad of Mummarn's slap, for bringing me back from those heights, for knocking me out of the god's mind. I didn't know what to do with so much knowledge.

"You would've thought she was proud as proud, handing over those boys," said Widow Hogtie softly.

"She held her head up," Widow Longhair agreed. "She held her back very straight."

I sat on the hammock between them. The moon shone down; the house behind us was silent for the moment.

"She looked like a chief, I thought. You can be proud of your mother, Currija. This"—Hogtie tipped her head toward the house—"this is all right, with only us to see it. But you don't want others to see you weeping and breaking."

"Oh, no," said Longhair.

"You don't want to be begging at those Church-men's knees."

"No, all they do is slap you away. Very hard to recover from."

"For the sons as well. You don't want that to be their last memory of you."

I cleared my throat. "They'll remember Mummarn well, all right."

They agreed, glad to hear me speak after my long silence, after Mummarn's upsetting sounds.

She started moving around again in there.

"Oh, blow," said Longhair. "I hoped she had gone to sleep."

All our belongings were out along the front wall; the house was an empty room where Mummarn couldn't hurt herself. She wailed again, the wail that rose from somewhere deeper than her own body and ran across my scalp like tree rats. Hogtie and Longhair leaned in around me. Charger lifted his head from Liklik's side and crooned, and we had to laugh a little.

"As if he's saying, 'Ooh, I know how you feel!' " said Hogtie.

"He's a good dog," said Longhair.

But then Mummarn screamed inside, "Val-laaaaah! Bra-vaaaaah! My babies!" and I cried again, and Longhair with me. If only Mummarn would not say the names! I did not want to think of the boys. Last I had seen of them was dry-eyed Brava waving back to Mummarn as she stood straight and smiling at the end of the bridge, fraught-faced Valla fingering away tears as he looked over his shoulder. The Church-man had clothed his whole self as if to make himself dark like us, except for his white collar, which I remember; it bobbed away through the trees. Sour old Three-Plait had come with the man, to do the talking; each widow had hoped to see her husband in that task, but *of course they send the old bachelor*, Widow Split had said, *the only one that's* not *missed*. Three-Plait, with no beard at all and only that close-clipped hair, in the same hot black clothes—he had hurried after the Church-man as if he were afraid of us. The whole business had been so fast, like a hawk snatching up a fish and flying off.

"It was *good* that it was so fast," I said, still crying, nearly asleep against Longhair's shoulder. "It was easier to keep our dignity." *We will keep our dignity*, Mummarn had said, embracing the boys in the house before we went down to the bridge. *We will not shed a tear.* And they had nodded, blinking.

"Yes, just for that little while," said Hogtie.

Until Widow Split had called from across the gorge that they were passed into Broad Valley. Mummarn bent and broke then, and we all rushed in to catch her.

What happens to our offerings? I had asked Mummarn as we walked down the path from Pinnacle Cliff. *Does it eat them, too, like the house? Or do they fall out, into the sea?*

It carries them all the way up, said Mummarn. *Our offerings and our words are caught inside it like fish in a tide trap.*

I could tell from her face that she believed this. *And then?*

And then is not our concern. Mummarn had smiled down on me. She was quite dry-eyed then; I could not imagine her ever crying again. *The gods do what the gods will do. We have shown them our people: we have told them how things are for us and we have put in our plea. It's as much as we can do, here on the ground.*

I didn't smile back; I didn't laugh at her mistaken thoughts; I didn't say anything. I hardly knew what had happened; I hardly knew what I carried home inside my own skin. Suddenly I was not the same kind of creature as Mummarn, as anyone else alive that I knew. I was the kind that could learn to call the gods down from the sky and up from the sea, the bigger elder gods, not such small fry as we had seen today. And I would not need to hurt them with hooks, or construct fancy bait for them, or

147

build up my winding-muscles. All I need do was listen to and learn their songs. And if I sang well enough myself, I might ask anything of them—that they organize the Church away, for instance, that they bring the men back to our village of widows. Now that those things are accomplished, it's as if they were always meant to be. Back then, when I was little, before everything, I could hardly imagine what I might do.

Daughter of the Clay

Maybe the heating ducts brought the words to me from the other room. Maybe the secretive softness of the women's voices made my ears stretch to hear. I stopped trying to push the doll's arm through the narrow spangled sleeve. I lifted my head.

Are you not able *to have other children?* the visitor lady asked my mother.

Oh, I suppose I am able. *I'm afraid, though. That they would all turn out the same. Like Cerise.*

I stood up and coughed and dropped the doll—*threw down* the doll—so that they would stop talking, and they did. I wanted to run out of the apartment, down the stairs round and round, out into the park and under the fresh-leafed trees, around the lake screaming until I was exhausted, until I forgot what I'd heard.

I closed my bedroom door on the silence outside, and propped my chair under the handle. I closed my blind on the sunny, breezeless open window so that it was as dark in my room as I could make it. I went to bed, all in my clothes, pulling the covers over my head. It was hot, but I made an airhole and I lay there and I tried not to exist.

My mother came and turned the door handle. "Cerise? Cerise, darling?" She tried to sound affectionate, because her visitor was there.

I put my head out of the bedclothes and said, "Please go away. Please leave me alone."

They left me. Later, when the lady had left, my mother tried again. "Cerise, open this door! What do you mean, locking your mother out!"

"Please leave me alone," I said in the same chilly way, and again she left me. Which was what I'd asked for, but not at all what I wanted.

The long afternoon went by. The blind dimmed with evening and the sounds of cars passing and people walking slowed and became more random and echoing. I lay in my sweat, half stifled, awaiting stifling night.

My father came home and there was quiet argument. Then the door handle again. "Sweetness?" he said. "Will you let me in? I know you're upset. Let me in and we can talk. I'm thinking maybe you need a hug right now? Maybe some dinner?"

I had not cried until then. "No, please go away," I said—I could use the same clear, calm voice, even through the tears. I was going to stay in here forever, hungry and unwanted. He would never hug me again.

He tried several more times during the evening.

"Please," I finally said, because it was true. "I'm sleeping." And he left me alone.

Deep in that night a noise woke me—some rustling-winged insect landing nearby. I had fought free of the sheet and quilt in my sleep; I turned my head on the damp pillow and opened my burning eyes. There it was, outside the swinging blind, on the sill: rustle-rustle, scrape.

I sat up. I was hungry. I am a solid girl with a good appetite, and I felt hollow and unbalanced. (My grandmother: *She eats everything I put in front of her. It's marvelous.* My mother: *Hmm. Yes, marvelous.* My grandmother: *While you were always so picky.*)

The blind swung in, and the small person squatting on the sill showed clearly against the city-lit clouds. She had thin dark arms and legs, and wore a ragged garment patterned like a Tiffany lampshade. Her head was like a praying mantis's, with bulging eyes at the top corners and a pointed chin. She smoked a pipe with a tiny bowl and a long, curved stem. The spicy smoke made my mind sit up and gasp and fumble after the memory that matched the smell.

"You're a fairy!" I said.

I saw two little puffs of smoke as she snorted before the blind swung back and covered her. I raised it quickly; she was still there.

"You have forgotten all your old language." Her voice was brittle as a cricket's.

"What language?"

"Ha," she said. " 'Fairy' language, you would call it. If I told you the word, you would not hear it."

"Try," I said urgently. "Please."

"I tried," she rattled. "Your ears are all fleshly now, all blood and gristle and little hairy hairs; you hear nothing." She sucked hard on the pipe and pushed the coal into it until her fingertip glowed.

"When you say 'now'—when you say I've 'forgotten' . . ."

She blew three tiny smoke rings, then sighed out the rest of the lungful of smoke. "I am not what you would call a Good Fairy. I wouldn't be here if I were. I don't talk and connect and orient. People can work it out for themselves, I reckon."

"Work what out?" I said. "And what if their brains are all blood and gristle, too, and they can't?"

She knocked out the pipe against the sill, with a shower of sparks, and stuck it away in the thin black frizz of her hair. She spread out her wings, which were like a dragonfly's, and groomed them quickly with her black arms.

"You're a Clay-Daughter," she said.

"A what-daughter?"

"Clay. Clay. You can't tell me you never noticed how rounded and mud-colored you are."

"But what *is* a Clay-Daughter?"

She was poised to fly off. "You were a swappee. You belong in 'Fairyland.' But nay, your flesh-twin is there instead, going all to Clay. Somebody threaded the pair of you, back and forth and back between the lands, to make this slip-through that I've just used." *Shirr*, went her wings, and she backed off the sill into the air.

"Stop!" I cried. "Tell me! My 'flesh-twin'—how do I find her?"

The fairy laughed, a noise like flakes of rust rubbing together.

"The way I came, it's still soft. But I never told you, is that clear? I'm not a Fixer; I've no business putting you to rights."

And she zoomed away between the buildings.

"Cerise?" The door handle moved again. "Are you all right? Did you call out for us?"

"No!" I said in the clear, calm voice. I leaped for the bed. "I'm sleeping! I'm fine!"

"Are you sure?"

I burrowed into the nest of bedclothes . . . *ever noticed how rounded and mud-colored* . . . Down and down I crawled, wanting to bury myself right at the bottom and never be dragged out. *You belong in 'Fairyland.'* The bed became very long, or I became very small, because I couldn't seem to reach the end of it. And it was warm down here, even beyond where my feet could have warmed it. And the folds of the sheet around me felt sticky. And there was light up ahead, as if I were in a cave, crawling toward the cave mouth. Had my father dislodged the chair somehow, pushed the door open, and turned on the light? And why was it—more than sticky, it was slippery, and I was slithering along it toward the light, toward the noise—

"Oh!"

Out I fell, into a party. Fairies danced in a whirl of black limbs and colored rags. No, not fairies—the nearest fleshly word for them was *zithers*, but the *z* and the *th* were Interland sounds, and couldn't really be said with a mouth. A man, a fleshly man, full-sized, bone-thin, staring-eyed, played the fiddle among them, wild music in a complicated joke of changing keys, and the *zithers* sang and shouted up to him, and swung from his waist-length hair.

I had fallen from a hole in a clay bank. Weeds curtained it, drooping from a rock lip above, where a roughly shaped stone stood on end. High above, all around, tall, thick trees blocked out most of the sky, which was lightening toward dawn. Down here, the *zithers'* eyes and clothing lit the dance, as did some frail red lanterns that were strung through the undergrowth.

"Come, lumpen!" someone chirped at my elbow. "Join the throng! Dawn is near and dancing time is dying."

Carefully I stood. My mouth waited for the old, lost phrases to form. "I did not come here to dance," I managed to say.

The *zither* spun away into the dark whirlpool around the fiddler. Wings flashed mauve and green and crimson in the spidery whirling; eyes scrolled lines of light across the forest floor. Some danced and some milled about; some embraced at the edges of the dance floor and out among the trees; tiny pottery cups lay tipped and smashed beside a broken barrel.

I gritted my teeth against the buzz and veer of the music, and picked my way around the crowd, checking for *zithers* with every step—the thought of their thin black limbs cracking underfoot filled me with horror. I knew where to go: follow the line of the clay; where there is a choice, take the downward way.

I walked free of the dance and the dizzying lights, free of the magic that hung in a cloud over that clearing, smelling of cloves and altering any brain that came near. Here it was dark and quiet and my own senses spoke to me truly, of the clay winding ahead to my home, of the soft ongoing groan of tree life and the gentle festivity of dark leaves, of beasts that slept like furred lamps here and there, in logs, underground, or folded small into nests and tree cavities overhead.

I worked my tongue against the roof of my mouth; it came away a little, like melting chocolate but without taste. My hands were damp and soft, too; I examined them in the dimness. A twig scraped across one and took some of my clay. I felt the scraped line in the back of my hand, but it did not hurt, and it would not last. My hair was heavy and flat against my shoulders.

Down I went, and the forest cast ever thicker nets above me. Deep down ahead, where the clay slanted into the earth next to the water, was where I'd find my people. I was warm with walking; they would be cool from the night, barely able to speak or think.

"Cerise?" I called softly, remembering my fleshly mouth. Out under a spreading screen of branches I walked onto the stream bank, and there they were, their mouths agape and fingers glued together in sleep. Some were as yet only emergent, welded to the clay wall or leaning on fixed feet; the fully formed ones, who like me could move about, could try the different foods of the world, maybe, or make their marks upon rock slab and tree bark, these sat or lay curled on their sides on the ground. All my blunt-headed family sagged and snored here, pale in the dawn dimness, and tiny others hung dormant, invisible in the Clay-mass, awaiting their time.

"Cerise?"

Through this strange museum of my selves I browsed. This one had a stone lodged in its forehead, that one a pattern of mineral streaks laid in its surface; each was at a different stage of formation, but none was as formed as I, as detailed in shape and surface as a fleshly person.

Except one.

"Cerise?"

She crouched on top of a low cliff of clay, her eyes glittering. "Why'djou call me that?" she said.

"Because it is your name," I said. "Your real name, in the fleshly world, where you began."

She climbed down the cliff. Her limbs were longer and finer than anyone's here, although clearly made of clay. She peered at me with my own face, at my clay hair, at my fingers, which were shorter and blunter than hers, but had the same pearly nails.

"Who am I in this place?" I whispered. "What do they call you?"

"Shorghch," she said. Of course. Shorghch. It was all coming back to me.

Now the stream's chuckles and the breathing of the clay people were not the only sounds. Faint sighs and moans moved them; a few stretched and turned. *Who's this one?* said someone dazedly.

"Come," I said to Cerise. "I will show you the way to your home."

I took her cool hand and led her back along the bank, up the hill. Dawn was opening the forest around us; high in the trees birds shook out their feathers and called in the first sunlight, though it stayed dark and damp down here.

"What is it like," Cerise said, "my home?"

"You'll remember," I said, "just as I remember this place. It will be easy for you, just as it was difficult here. All you will have to do is smile, and tend your hair, and keep your room tidy, and—"

"I will have hair? Like a fox? What is a *room*?"

157

"Don't worry," I said. "Everything will be clear to you. You'll have a beautiful mother and a very kind father and—"

Something crumbled inside me, distantly, interestingly. It was like watching an apartment building collapse, an apartment building at the far end of our street, in which no one lived that we knew. I turned to watch Cerise stepping sprightly up the slope. "They will be different with you. They will be happy with you."

Her clay hair already shone better than mine ever had. "What is *mother?*"

"You will see soon enough. You will know."

A man cried out ahead of us, up high in the clearing.

"It's that fiddler," I said. "Come along; we're nearly there."

He shouted out more as we climbed, in a foreign language, a fleshly language—German, I thought. Was that the name of it? My Cerise-language was coming unstuck in my head, suspended like so much soil in water.

Cerise pulled on my hand. "I don't like him," she muttered. "I don't want to go near."

"We must," I said. "The way home is right there."

"Are you sure?"

In this better light I saw her necklace of twined thorn twigs, with red berries spiked on each thorn tip. *How clever!* my mother would have said. *So pretty, and it keeps the thorns from scratching you!* There was a ring, too, that matched, a cluster of four berries against her rough beige skin.

"I'm certain," I said. "It won't take long, don't worry."

The fiddler raved and threw himself about on the bare

dance floor, shouting in his German. He had what looked like shards of Easter egg in his hands, and he stopped to suck ferociously on these now and then. They did not break or diminish— Oh, they were barrel staves, and he was sucking the last traces of nectar from them.

Cerise was right up against my back, huddling down because she was taller than me and trying to hide. "Make him go away," she said.

He saw us, the fiddler, and jumped to his feet. "Mongrels!" He pointed two staves at us. "What are you? Not fish, nor fleisch are you neither!"

"Quickly, Cerise!" I pushed her past him—though shorter, I was much heavier than this long-boned girl. She whimpered and resisted, but she went.

The fiddler came after us, shouting; he threw barrel wood at us, and nectar cups. "Ow!" said Cerise, but my skin was past feeling any stings.

I pushed her through the screen of weeds under the marker rock. There was the hole, rimmed with wet clay. A warm breath came from it, smelling of the lavender room scent my mother sprayed around my bedroom. (*How can this room smell of* earth, *Cerise?* she would say, spraying, bothered. *We're on the sixth floor! Have you tracked dirt in on your shoes? Show me!*) A tiny distant voice came out, too, loaded with fear and grief, which I recognized as my father's: *Ceri-i-ise!*

Cerise balked. "In *there*? I won't *fit*!"

The fiddler snatched the curtain of weeds aside. His face flowered into joy at the sight of the clay hole. He dived for it.

"Stop him, Cerise!" I shouted. "Catch his other leg!"

She caught it and pulled. Her hair was already separating into silky strands. The berries at her throat were darkening and changing to faceted surfaces. She wore the face my mother wore when strangers asked her for money on the street, the *I-should-not-have-to-endure-this* face.

Still, she was strong; she still had some Clay in her. And I was slabby and heavy now. Together we pulled the fiddler out of the hole. Clay smeared him down to the waist and squeezed out of his fists. His clayed face opened and he bawled in protest.

Now Cerise knew what to do. She ran up the length of him. She crouched on his shoulders and cleared his claggy hair from the opening. Neatly she inserted her joined hands in the slip-through, her silky head, her narrow frame. She pulled up her long legs and kicked off from the fiddler's head. The last I saw were her dirty feet slipping away, pointed like a ballerina's. (*No, point them, Cerise! Is that as far as they will point? It can't be!*)

My ears popped; the scent of cloves puffed on the air. I lay across the fiddler's legs, pinning him down as he rolled and raved and wept and beat his clayey fists against the solid bank.

"I had a mother once—and a father, too."

Zithers don't understand this, and neither do the Clay. *Zither* mothering and fathering is quite a different thing—a matter of feeding and magic and mild torture—and the Clay, of course, are born of earth and know no parent.

"There was this fleshly *thing*, this fleshly *tendency* they expected of me. I watched real children do it, but I could not bring it out of myself."

Gerken sighs. She would move away were she not still anchored in the stream bank.

"The father could tend toward me like a real one, somehow. But the mother—I don't know, at the end there I think she was not even trying, really. She did not even touch me anymore."

Gerken nods, though she cannot know what I mean. "It's terrible that you can't change back properly, once you've been even a little bit Flesh."

Byredy comes up the bank. "Accidentally I caught this extra fish," she says. "You might as well have it, Shorghch."

"Mm, a plump one," says Gerken. "And still kicking, look."

"Yes, and when you pull that foot free you can have some. Here, Shorghch."

I hold the fish around the middle and watch it gape and bend.

"She is reminiscing," says Gerken to Byredy.

"About her fleshly time?" Byredy rolls her eyes, her face full of fish.

"If you are tired of it, I won't continue." I turn my back on them and bite into the fish. If only I could tell about it better!

When she was bent over something—something else besides me (a letter, maybe, or a telephone)—I could see what they meant when they said my mother was a great beauty. Sometimes my father looked at her and was trying, trying to make right what was wrong—which was me, of course, which he could not make right, which only I could, which only I *did!*—and the reason he tried, I think, was in service to her beauty, because even *he* must not like the way her mouth pinched up when I was there, or the way her eyes widened and looked about for a reason to go out of the room, or the things that happened to her voice.

There was a night, though, when I lay very nearly fleshly in my bed, and they came home laughing and then hushed themselves and came into my room. And in the dim light they could not see the Clayness of me, could only hear my breathing, see how small my shape slept, know that I meant no ill. And she leaned down in her furs and fashions and scent, and he in his vast coat—I could smell snow melting into the shoulders—and each kissed me, he on my temple, she on my cheek.

They are like mineral stains, those kiss prints, or like gouges in my clay too deep to refill. Every so often a *zither* cocks her head at me and says, *What is it about you, then?*—so others can see the prints, too. But what is the point of telling a *zither*, only to see her thin-shouldered shrug? Why would I tell anyone here that, a little and forever, I am Cerise with her silky hair and ruby necklace, and that she, though kisses rain upon her for all her mortal life, though our mother combs her and lullabies her and gives her baby sisters and brothers for her playthings, will always have a whiff of Clay about her?

Why? There is no reason to keep telling it, over and over. I did what I did. Only *zithers* can undo it, and they never do anything for the asking, only for their own selves and desires. Better to stay silent, better always to stay silent, to sit on my bottom among the Clay and fill my mouth with fish.

Acknowledgments

The author acknowledges the following sources of ideas, images, and references for these stories:

"Baby Jane" probably wouldn't have happened if I hadn't read Lynne Reid Banks's Indian in the Cupboard series, or gone to Jo Creagh's birth classes in 1988 before Jack was born.

"Monkey's Paternoster" was directly inspired by a documentary about the Hanuman langur monkeys in the Indian city of Jodhpur, probably *Warriors of the Monkey God*, directed by Phil Chapman (1999).

"A Good Heart" came about after I went to two classes in February and March 2005: Gillian Polack's weekend course "Understanding the Medieval World" at the New South Wales

Writers' Centre, and Sybil Jack's WEA class "Medieval Forests in Fact and Myth."

"Winkie" and "Mouse Maker" were both inspired by my reading Marina Warner's *No Go the Bogeyman: Scaring, Lulling, and Making Mock* (London: Chatto and Windus, 1998). Warner only had to mention Wee Willie Winkie in the context of bogeymen and I knew there was a story there; when I went back to check the reference, I realized that the picture on page 35 by "Dicky" Doyle, from around 1890, of a very tall bogeyman carrying a basket full of children down a hill toward a thick miasma, must have also imprinted itself on my mind. Warner also quoted a caption Goya wrote for a sketch of a heretic he made some time around 1820, when he was preoccupied with the Spanish Inquisition: "They put a gag on her because she talked . . . [and hit her about the head . . . because she knew how to make mice]." Robert Hughes also quotes this caption in *Goya* (New York: Alfred A. Knopf, 2004), and adds that mouse-making was "a not uncommon charge in witch hunts at the height of the Inquisition."

"A Feather in the Breast of God" comes from owning the budgies named in the dedication; the Leonard-Drummond family's cat Manga, who disappeared for several months but came back and took up residence again, was another trigger.

"Hero Vale" is about a place that is very like the Wood Between the Worlds in C. S. Lewis's *The Magician's Nephew*.

The foundation for "Under Hell, Over Heaven" was laid during my Catholic primary school education in the 1960s, in teachings about Limbo. The new pope is about to revise the Catholic Church's beliefs regarding this place.

My first notes for "Forever Upward" read: "An island community. Colonised by churchpeople who give all the power to the men. All the religion, too. The Free Church is a church on a string, made of paper, unreeled from the top of a cliff, occasionally, for the use of women, curmudgeons and solitaires."

I never would have written "Daughter of the Clay" if I hadn't first read "Remember Me" by Nancy Farmer, in Sharyn November's *Firebirds* anthology (New York: Penguin, 2003): "She spent hours sewing weird dresses that made her look like she ate whale sandwiches for lunch. They were in really dead colors—mud, algae, pond scum. That kind of thing. Once she made a pair of hot pants in *toad*." And I never would have thought of the title without having read about the Clayr in Garth Nix's Abhorsen trilogy.

I would also like to gratefully acknowledge the Literature Board of the Australia Council for the Arts, who supported this work with a fellowship.